Man In The Water

Jon Hill

Banzai Press

For contact information visit; www.jonhillwrites.com

ISBN: 9780578958699

For Matt
Thanks for all the years of friendship.
Someday, we'll get that movie made.
Fargo, my friend.

GET A FREE BOOK!

Visit www.jonhillwrites.com and join the mailing list for your free novella! This is the only way you can read this story. It is not for sale! Unless you happen to find some of the rare paperbacks that have been strategically left behind at certain beach houses!

1

STACEY GREEN SPIT A mouthful of toothpaste into the sink before rinsing her mouth with a handful of water from the faucet. As she placed the purple toothbrush back in the ceramic toothbrush holder, rejoining it with the other two—one red, one blue—she looked at her reflection in the mirror and stared. They were actually doing it.

A chorus of repeated blows began sounding against the bathroom door, shattering her thoughts.

"Yes?" she answered, brushing a blonde string of hair away from her eyes.

"Mommy!" A muffled cry came back.

She opened the door to see Joseph standing there with a cookie in one hand and a black marker in the other.

"Oh, Joseph." She sighed. He'd gotten his hands mixed up again, and instead of cookie crumbs lingering on his lips, there were heavy black lines tracing them. She bent over and picked the four-year-old up into her arms. "Jack!"

Her husband poked his head around the corner. "Yeah—ah, crap." He stepped toward them. "Come here, buddy." He took Joseph from Stacey's arms. "Where the heck did he get a cookie?"

"He mixed his hands up again."

"That's gotta be some kind of symptom of something, right? I mean—"

She cut him off. "You left the marker on the table again, didn't you?"

"What marker?"

She shook her head.

"Come on," he said, "go finish getting ready." He pinched her butt, and she screamed.

They traded places, her heading off to the bedroom, him taking a washcloth from the cabinet beneath the sink.

"When's your mother gonna be here?" Jack called after her. "We're gonna miss the flight!"

"I'll call her!" her voice came back.

He turned his attention to his son. "All right, Joe, let's see if we can fix your face before Grandma gets here and has Child Services on the phone."

"Oh!" he exclaimed, excited. "Can I go?"

"Go where?"

"Child Services!"

Jack laughed. "Sounds fun, huh?"

"Is it like a park? Like Sesame Place? Is it just for kids?" The prospect of going somewhere that was just for kids had Joseph's eyes gleaming with wonder. Whatever his little mind had conjured up must have been something spectacular.

Jack scrubbed the ink off with the washcloth, Joseph's lips and cheeks pulling and stretching all over the place, distorting his face like one of those carnival mirrors and making Jack smile. "I don't think you'd like it very much. Not unless you want to end up in Lebanon as some sheik's boy toy."

"Jack!" Stacey protested from the bedroom.

"What? It happens. Kids are taken in and disappear, turning up years later in —"

"Jack! He's *four*!"

"Exactly," he argued. "Probably the prime age for—"

A shoe came flying down the hallway and banged against the bathroom door.

"I'm warning you," Stacey's voice followed.

"Okay, okay." He looked at Joseph, the boy's lips still reaching for his ears beneath the hard strokes of the washcloth. "Sheesh." He winked.

Joseph looked confused. And then he asked, "Is Grandma going to run away with me now?"

Evidently, Joseph had overheard a few of his father's remarks concerning the mother-in-law's disdain for certain of his parenting techniques.

"Well," Jack said, biting the inside of his cheek while thinking, "if she tries it, just go along with her. Best not to tip her off right away. Make her think you want to go with her. You'll have more freedom that way. And then, when you have a chance, take her phone and call me. You still have my number memorized, right?"

He nodded.

"Good. So call me, and I'll come get you."

"Promise?"

"Promise."

As the last black smear disappeared from Joseph's face, he broke out in a smile. "That's silly, Daddy. Grandma can't run. She's too old."

Jack laughed. "Don't you dare tell *her* that. She'll think you got it from me. I'll wake up one morning missing my thumbs." He wiggled them for Joseph to see, provoking another fit of laughter from the blond wavy-haired boy. "Did you know Grandma has a fetish for thumbs? She puts them in her freezer," he whispered.

Joseph screamed with laughter. "No, she doesn't!" Then his blue eyes grew as serious as any four-year-old set of peepers could. "Daddy?"

"What?"

"Why are you and Mommy going away?"

He rinsed the washcloth off and sat down on the toilet, taking Joseph up onto his lap. "Well, like I told you before, sometimes mommies and daddies just need a little break, to spend some alone time and relax for a while." He'd told him this more than a dozen times over the last week, but for some reason the explanation just wouldn't satisfy the inner workings of his young analytical mind.

With a sudden sadness glossing over sober eyes, Joseph asked, "You and Mommy are coming back, right?"

"What? Of course we're coming back!" He squeezed him tight. "It's just some special grown-up time for Mommy and Daddy, that's all. Do you understand? We could never, *ever* leave you." But before Jack could further dissect the psychology of the boy's concern, a beep sounded from the driveway.

"Grandma!" Joseph cried. He hopped down and sprinted to the front door, his wiry body flailing with joy despite his fear that Grandma would run away with him someday—*if* she could run.

Jack tossed the washcloth into the clothes basket behind the door and walked to the bedroom.

"Hey, what do you think about this?" Stacey asked, holding a skimpy piece of pink lingerie up to her shoulders. She puckered her lips and tossed her hair.

Jack kicked the door shut with his heel. "What do I think?" He walked toward her, hunger burning in his eyes.

She laughed when he picked her up off the floor and pressed her against the bedroom wall. "Stop." She giggled. "My mom is here!"

He dropped her and turned away. "Yeah, that'll do it."

"Oh, come on," she said, throwing the sexy apparel at his back. "My mother is not that bad."

He raised his eyebrows but swallowed whatever remark had sprouted as a response. "Come on. We're cutting it close."

After stealing a quick glance at the clock resting on the table beside their king-size bed, Stacey squinted at him. "We've got two hours."

"Yeah, assuming the TSA doesn't spend half that time probing for your nuclear tampon." He cocked his head to the side. "You're leaving it here, right?"

"It's locked away safe and sound."

"Locked away where?"

She shook her head.

"Hey, I am not the one probing people like Nazi thugs, my dear."

"Well, be sure to call them that when they have your hands against the wall and your legs spread apart. I'd like to see where they tase you. But you'd better understand, I'll be on that boat with or without you."

"Okay, Joshua Tree."

She walked to the corner of the room where their suitcases sat packed and waiting. "Hey, you're not still on the No-Fly List, are you?"

Shock burst across his face. "There's a No-Fly List?"

Stacey laughed and, hearing her mother being greeted by Joseph at the front door, motioned for her husband to grab their bags. "Come on then, Jerry."

Jerry was his nickname, taken from Mel Gibson's character in the movie *Conspiracy Theory*, that flick with Julia Roberts and Patrick Stewart. Jerry Fletcher. He'd earned the name by publicly stating that Bin Laden was a CIA creation forged during the Afghan war with the Russians. That radical Islam itself could be blamed on blowback from Operation Ajax in 1953 when, for oil, the CIA overthrew the only democratic leadership Iran would probably ever see. But even though it was now common knowledge, the Jerry name still stuck.

However, more than being a conspiracy theorist and a programmed CIA assassin with a background in MK-ULTRA, DELTA, or NAOMI, Jerry was also a pretty goofy guy. It was what made the movie so fun to watch. So the nickname wasn't meant to be a "tinfoil hat" remark, but rather a "you're so cute and goofy with your crazy theories" statement.

Of course, many so-called "conspiracy theories" had a habit of turning out to be true with the declassification of certain documents. But despite the truth of the matter, the reputation of the "theorist" never received public acquittal, and the corporate media would report the long-awaited proof as if they discovered it and hadn't rained hell fury on those who had been reporting it for years. The Gulf of Tonkin, for instance. Or the USS *Liberty*. So, despite whatever he'd claimed as conspiracy becoming common knowledge overnight with a declassified document, he would always be Jerry.

It was their friend Ivan, though, who should really have such a designation. He was the legit alternate historian, his mind a sponge, Russian genius his background. But he wasn't cute, goofy, or crazy. So "Jerry" was left to Jack while Ivan remained, well...Ivan.

But in truth, Jack loved the name. He wasn't entirely sure why. Maybe because Jerry had been right. Maybe because, in the end, he saved the day and got the girl. He didn't know. He just knew that he smiled inwardly whenever Stacey used it. It was a pet name, a name that encompassed their understanding of each other, her endearment toward him no matter what. The world and all of its thoughts be damned, he was her Jerry. And he could live with that forever.

Absorbing the nickname as he always did, he smiled and started shimmying toward her, singing Frankie Valli's "Can't Take My Eyes off You" in his best Mel Gibson impersonation.

She smiled. "I think a two-week cruise will be good for my Jerry."

My Jerry. Mel never had it so good.

"Mommy! Daddy! Grandma's here!" Joseph's voice rebounded throughout the house.

Picking up the bags, Jack asked Stacey, "You're sure he'll be okay with your mom for two weeks?"

Her thin lips twisted into a mischievous grin. "Let's go to the Bahamas."

"Aye, aye." He handed her the pink lingerie. "Maybe put it away before your mom sees it."

"You don't want her trying it on?"

He looked horrified. "You think she would?"

"Maybe if we asked."

"Why would we do that?"

"You're right. Poor Joseph."

"*Joseph*?"

She nudged him toward the door. "Yeah, imagine what it would be like seeing your granny showing off Victoria's secret...and then being left alone with her for two weeks."

He opened the door and started down the hallway, then turned back to face her. "Wow. I think I need therapy."

"Therapy for what?" a voice suddenly asked.

"Oh, shh—" He spun around and came face-to-face with his mother-in-law. With a huge feigned grin, he waved a hello. "Hi, Viki. Been standing there long?"

His mother-in-law, Viktoriya Arsov, had one firm hand on his son's head, her skinny fingers woven through his blond hair, and the other clenched in a fist against one of her slender hips. And though her face was all smiles, her eyes told him that she had heard everything—just as she always seemed to. That piercing gray gaze gave him the creeps, and he shivered beneath its judgment.

Clapping his hands, he said, "Okay then! Great! Well, it's time for us to go. We appreciate you doing this for us, Viki. Really..."

She waved him off. "It is the least that I can do for my precious daughter. She should enjoy herself before the mortal chaos of—"

"Yeah...thanks, Viki," he interrupted, moving past her and taking the bags to the door.

"Oh, my dear child," Mrs. Arsov said, her thick Russian accent decorating the address as she wrapped her strong but skinny arms around her. "Enjoy yourself. Everything is taken care of here. You don't need to worry about anything. Just... be careful."

Jack stood in the front doorway, watching mom-in-law whisper her farewell exchange. Despite all his teasing, she wasn't completely unattractive. She was aged, and long mysterious years of some unknown past had etched heavily into her features, but there was still a whisper of former beauty left clinging to her rusted frame. Tall and lean, she was also muscular and strong, and she carried herself like some kind of countess. That was probably the most disconcerting part, the strange sense of authority that seemed to demand fear and respect without any declaration as to why. And Stacey either didn't notice it, or she pretended not to. But whenever Viktoriya cast her mighty gaze on him, he felt like Cinderella before her evil stepmother. He wondered what life in Russia had been like, and what had made her leave the Motherland.

Joseph walked over and stood beside him. "Come here, Joe." Jack dropped to his knees and spread his arms wide, inviting his son into a reassuring embrace. "I love you so much," he whispered into his ear. "No matter what, I'll always love you." He wasn't sure why he had just said that. "Be really good for Grandma, okay? We'll be back before you know it. And we'll go to the Yankees game just like I promised."

"Can I get cotton candy?"

"Sure you can." He kissed him on the forehead and felt his eyes begin to water. It would be two weeks before they were together again, a span of time that suddenly felt endless. They squeezed each other tight, and Jack could tell that Joseph didn't want to let go. "It's okay, buddy. We'll be back. Hey, I'll find something cool to bring you, okay?" He felt Joseph nod against his shoulder.

When they separated, Jack standing to his full six feet two inches and Joseph his little three feet five inches, Joseph stated, "I love you, Daddy."

Jack tried to keep the tears at bay. Not only would it be two weeks, but it would also be the first time they'd be apart from each other at all. "Remember," he teased, "if she tries running..." He winked, and Joseph grinned.

Stacey separated from her mother and came over to give her own sad goodbye. Jack didn't want to witness this one. He took the luggage to the car, where he would be spared the tear-filled display.

Jack started the Hyundai Sonata and looked in the rearview mirror, noting the absence of the car seat that had been at home in the reflection for the last four years. It would be transferred to Viktoriya's car, God help them all.

Five minutes later, Stacey was sliding into the passenger seat beside him, wiping her eyes.

"You're sure he'll be okay with her?" Jack asked once more.

She nodded, and they backed down the driveway.

Jack beeped the horn, and they both waved to Joseph. He was waving from the front door, Grandma towering behind him.

Stacey blew them a kiss.

2

THE TSA HADN'T FONDLED them or shipped them off to some black site where the CIA could freely torture them under Rendition laws supposedly spawned to protect their liberties. No waterboarding, no electrocuting Jack's genitals, and no sleep-deprivation tactics. In fact, the TSA agents hadn't even pulled them out of line. And maybe Jack had pushed his luck a bit by singing out, "For the land of the freeeeee..." while walking through the radiation belts of the see-you-naked machines, but such luck had held fast. So far.

Jack recalled a story in Miami where an employee was made fun of after the scanners showed off his small genitalia during a practice session with the publically funded machines. He later beat the crap out of the instigator and was arrested the next day when he showed up for work. That was Miami, their destination.

And of course, there were the countless official complaints by women who believed they were sexually harassed, being made to go through the machines three and four times while men congregated in the viewing room to ogle. If there was any of that awaiting them in Miami, then the odds were good that he wouldn't be making the boat after all.

Jack put down the Koontz novel and squeezed Stacey's hand while looking out the window beside him. The clouds were large and puffy, and his eyes were inadvertently picking out cotton images. He could make out Colonel Sanders smiling at them, his head fixed atop a tall ladder that was being scaled by an octopus with the head of a pterodactyl. Dennis Rodman was strapped to the back of a walrus, and a naked mermaid with cow udders stood poised at home plate with a spiked mace. Closing his eyes to erase the scene, Jack wondered if it was a testament to how warped his mind was. Upon opening them again, he was relieved to see that only the ladder remained. He went to ask Stacey what it was that she saw, but she was asleep. His lips pulled adoringly, and he leaned his head back against the headrest, staring at her.

Stacey Arsov, daughter of the Russian widow Viktoriya... How the heck did they end up together? It was like one of those teen movies where the class loser ends up with the prom queen and then beats up the captain of the football team for added measure. Ridiculous. Yet here he was. Not that he had been the class loser, but a salesman from northeast Philly was close enough when held in comparison with her supermodel looks and brilliant wit. She was from another planet of status but for some reason had traded her citizenship for a life with him. Why? What did he have to offer her? Could it really just be love...or fate? Had Cupid sneezed while loosing his arrow? Or had Jack stumbled clumsily into his line of fire, intercepting adoration meant for the captain of the football team? He shrugged. Who cared? She was his, and he would never let her go. No matter what.

No. Matter. What.

A tear formed in the corner of his eye, and he forced the ensuing thoughts away. Instead, he chose to revisit the story of

Them, five years in the making and the best yet to come. He had to think that way. To do anything else would be to surrender, to give up. And that wasn't going to happen. They would fight until the last morsel of willpower was forcibly extracted from their collective soul.

It was a pleasant story, the story of Them, beginning almost six years ago with a single glance. Like destiny just set its crosshairs over his heart and pulled the trigger. That was it. No going back. She, on the other hand, needed a bit more than a single shot from an intergalactic sniper love-gun. Not much more, but enough to make him sweat it out all the way to the altar.

When they met, just three months before being married, Jack was working the same job he'd been working since graduating from Temple University, and Stacey had just moved into Philadelphia to take a job as an event organizer for a new outfit downtown. They'd met at a bar on a Friday night, and everything took off from there. Once they decided on marriage, there was nothing but Viktoriya standing in the way.

He had no brothers or sisters, his father had been an only child, and his mother's sister lived in Florida. As for his parents themselves...they'd died in a tragic car accident on Roosevelt Boulevard when he was just six years old, leaving him to be raised by the grandmother on his father's side. She had died his first year in college. The only family that he had left was his aunt in Florida and some cousins in California.

All Stacey had was her mother—the Russian countess. So after her eminence finally surrendered to fate's chorus of wedding bells, there was nothing to hinder them from "till death do us part."

Joseph was conceived shortly after, and upon his birth, their fairytale pact had been stamped with the eternal seal of shared responsibility...with a creation that had been perfectly orchestrated from two genetic makeups destined to be one. They had become more than lovers, more than husband and wife. They had become a family.

"I want a drink."

Jack opened his eyes, not realizing they'd fallen shut, and saw Stacey looking down the aisle for the stewardess.

"Bad dream?" he asked.

"The plane lost an engine, and we crashed in the Everglades. The survivors banded together and for three days were gnawed on by monster alligators. We died last with our intestines wrapped around each other and our stomachs floating like jellyfish in the water."

He blinked, then shot a furtive glance out the window. The open mouth of a large reptile floated toward them. "Make it two."

THE FLIGHT TO MIAMI was uneventful—the box cutter of all box cutters hadn't brought the nation to its knees, there were no mishaps into alligator-infested swamps, and the TSA hadn't rummaged through Stacey's goods. All in all, it had gone as well as could be hoped in today's world. And now here they were, floating on a ship in the middle of a blue nothing with two weeks of romance and unbridled passion on the horizon. *Oh yeah.*

Stacy stretched back on the deck chair, reclining in her bikini while dropping her own novel to the deck beside her.

Jack ran a hand through his short black hair and looked over, his eyes gliding over the terrain of his wife's body. Once he had the geography properly surveyed, he let his eyes flutter down to the title of her book. "*Simple Simon*, by Ryne Douglas Pearson. Hmm...never heard of him."

She closed her eyes, absorbing the warmth of the afternoon sun as the ocean breeze played with her hair. "You ever see the Bruce Willis movie *Mercury Rising*?"

He closed Koontz's *The House of Thunder* and squinted over the tops of his mirrored sunglasses. "Of course."

"This is the book the movie's based on. There's actually a whole series based on the character."

"I didn't know that."

"Book's much better." She moved the straps of her bikini down off her shoulders, her eyes still closed. "Remember that movie we saw in the theater with Nicolas Cage...*Knowing*?"

"Yeah, I loved that movie."

"He wrote the screenplay for it."

"Bruce Willis?"

The corner of her mouth rose into a smirk. "Nicholas Cage."

"Oh."

Without opening her eyes, she reached down and tapped the author's name with her finger.

"I actually read *Confessions*," he said.

"Mine?"

"Pearson's. But they weren't *his* confessions—"

"So you did hear of him?"

He smiled. "I love you."

She placed a hand on his thigh.

"Hey, watch it!" He brushed her hand away. "There's people around."

"Oh, like that's a major concern of yours." She pulled her top down further, exposing flesh that hadn't seen daylight in at least five years.

The section of the deck they were reclining on was packed with other sunbathers offering their skin as sacrifice to the solar system's fiery center. A couple of young women were lying on their stomachs a few chairs away, topless.

"What are you doing?" Jack asked her.

"What?"

"You're exposing yourself to all these strapping young men. They're liable to become jealous."

She ran a hand through her hair. "Won't that make you feel good? Men ten years younger than you jealous of the wife you were somehow able to catch?"

"Not while they're tossing me overboard as some kind of savage ritual aimed to impress you."

"Oh. Well, then maybe I just want your eyes on *my* melons and not theirs." She nodded to the topless college students.

"Oh, please. They have nothing on you." He opened the book.

"And how do you know that?"

He bit his lower lip. "I didn't—*don't* know...that. I...wait, what did you say? You talking about those people over there? They're men, aren't they?" He leaned forward, feigning to get a better look. "They're *wo*-men?"

"You're ridiculous," she responded. They looked like strippers with their perfect butts hanging out for every male to see. Their thongs were practically invisible between their tanned cheeks.

"I'll make you a deal," Stacey began, "take off your mirrored sunglasses, or I take off my top and let the frat boys woo me by tearing you to pieces and throwing your limbs to the sharks."

"Sharks?" Jack sat forward. "There's sharks out here?"

"It's the ocean, dear."

He took his sunglasses off and set his gaze on the blue seas. Some kind of island music was playing over the speaker system, and the serenity of it all made him sigh with satisfaction. He reached over and took Stacey's hand. "Am I really that old?" he wondered aloud, reflecting back on the "ten years younger" remark. Then he sifted further back through the conversation. "Hey, what did you mean, '*somehow* able to catch you'?"

"Don't worry about it, honey. If truth be told, I caught you."

3

"YOUR MOM DIDN'T SPARE any expense, did she?"

Jack was lying on the king-size bed, his fingers interlocked behind his head, taking in their suite. At the foot of the bed was a wall of floor-to-ceiling windows that stood looking out into the great blue unknown. The view captivated him. It was so vast and humbling that it almost scared him. Even aboard this enormous pleasure vessel, they were but a freckle on the rear end of a sand flea. The enormity of it made all the problems of twenty-first century man seem insignificant in some cosmological way. People, with all of their problems, died. Wars were fought and won, one generation's challenge gave way to the next...but this ocean was still here, completely indifferent to mankind's petty and insanity-driven issues.

Stacey walked in from the living room, and her stunning presence brought him out of his musings. No, death was not a petty concern. Whether nature cared about it or not, it was the most serious and sobering consideration of man. Death... It was what made life worth living, what made every day precious—it's limited supply the very source of its value. Just like any precious resource, the more common it is, the less value it has. Soul economics. And though we try as hard as we can to add more days to it, inflation hasn't been all that significant. Life was only common to those in power, who saw people as numbers born for their own ego; it was never a common thing to the individual person.

The problem, however, was being able to get the most out of those limited days when it looked as if the last grains of sand were about to tumble through the narrow waist of the hourglass. Especially when it seemed unfair, that time had come too soon to rob a loved one of so many unfulfilled hopes and dreams.

Like cancer.

Stacey sat down next to him, her gaze also locked on the rolling mystery they were floating on. "She has the money, and she just wants us—"

"You."

"—*me*," she corrected herself, "to enjoy myself before everything slips down the crapper."

He positioned himself up on an elbow and stroked her long hair. "It's gonna be okay."

She turned her eyes from the expanse and set them down on him, smiling sadly. Without a word, she reached down and grabbed his other hand. She held it tight.

It was true. According to the doctors, cancer had been detected in the aftermath of her last mammogram. Jack was half-convinced that it came from the mammograms themselves, as certain studies have shown. It was a conversation they'd had a bit too late and was a moot point now. But it didn't even matter because they were going to beat it. The only question was *how*? They were both highly skeptical of all the traditional treatments, and there was no way she was going to spend the last four years of her life begging for death, looking like some sixty-pound extra from the set of *The Walking Dead.* There were other options available, and they were going to investigate them all before starting down that gauntlet of misery.

So, as a gift from his mother-in-law, this two-week cruise was to be their calm before the storm, and though it was never put into words, perhaps their last chance to be happy together.

Leaning over, Stacey kissed him on the cheek while sliding her hand up his leg. Then she got up and began undressing as she left the room.

Jack watched her leave and had to fight hard and quick to reinforce the dam that was keeping all his worry at bay. There was plenty of time to be concerned later. For now, they were going to forget about cancer and enjoy themselves in ways they hadn't in a long time.

He reached over for the television remote and turned on the big flat-screen that hung on the wall beside the bed. The channel showed the ship's progress, a red dot moving slowly against a map. The tip of Florida was still in view, as were the approaching Bahamas. They were about sixty miles away from Miami now.

Stacey entered the room again, now wearing some kind of transparent robe thingy. As she opened the door and stepped out onto the balcony, Jack stared in amazement at his wife's beauty. Over the last four years, she had managed to regain all she'd lost in childbearing, her body a finer piece of sensuous art than it had ever been before. She stood with her back to him, the wind blowing her veil open and back like a cape. There was no one but him to see her nakedness since the balcony was privately set apart from the rest of the staterooms. Only Neptune could see her. Or a submariner at his periscope.

He stared at her for another five minutes before she turned and walked back in.

"Want to take a shower before dinner?"

He was out of the bed faster than a startled frog off a lily pad.

4

THE SUN WAS SETTING behind Stacey's head, highlighting her golden hair and casting a radiant halo. The black dress she was wearing was formfitting and revealed enough to attract even the purest of eyes. Jack didn't need to worry about that, though. Everything he saw was his. He recalled a verse from somewhere in Proverbs—a verse he and his junior high friends had no trouble committing to memory back in Father Jacob's class. *Let thy fountain be blessed: and rejoice with the wife of thy youth. Let her be as the loving hind and pleasant roe; let her breasts satisfy thee at all times: and be thou ravished always with her love.* He was satisfied all right. And though his eyes might wander from time to time, it was only because he was a curious human being, not because he wished for something more than he already had.

"What are you smirking at?" Stacey asked.

He didn't realize his thoughts had made it to his face. "I was just reciting some scripture."

She rolled her eyes in mock disgust.

"Communist," he quipped.

"From Russia with love, baby." She winked at him, leaning forward on the table and giving him more to take in.

"'Thy two breasts are like two young roes that are twins, which feed among the lilies.'"

"Really?"

"'This thy stature is like to a palm tree, and thy breasts to clusters of grapes.'"

"Tell me more." She slid the menu over, ignoring a group of people squeezing past her chair and sitting at a table beside them.

"'I said, I will go up to the palm tree, I will take hold of the boughs thereof: now also thy breasts shall be as clusters of the vine, and the smell of thy nose like apples.'"

"Apples, huh?"

He shrugged. "Wisest guy to ever live. Had a thousand wives."

"That's a lot of breasts."

"Two thousand, I believe."

She leaned back and brought the menu up, blocking his view of her clusters. "A theologian… I had no idea. Shall we debate over dinner?"

"About the smell of your nose?"

"The existence of God."

He moved his gaze to the waters resting just over her shoulder. "I'd rather not. You know what they said about the *Titanic*."

"You think God sunk the boat because some idiot said that He *couldn't* sink it?"

"Idiot? I would think you'd agree."

"That God couldn't sink a boat? That implies that there is a God who can't sink a boat. So he's an idiot. Secondly, if there was a God, then He could certainly sink anything He wanted. So he's an idiot twice over."

He leaned back and studied her. "You're my theology. Beauty, love… How can I behold you and not believe in a Creator?"

She smiled. "I love it when you're naive. It's so sweet."

Jack loved the quipping and did his part to ensure that it was exercised often; their differing views on spiritual matters a source of mock-contention that they found entertaining.

When Jack's parents died, his grandmother had taken him in, determined to see him raised right. A religious woman if there ever was one, it was only natural that Jack ended up with a Christian education (rather than, as Grandmom said, "the propaganda the State's shoveling into the youth these days"—though there had certainly been a form of propaganda within his Christian education, too).

Good old Grandmom, how he missed her. She died the day after he turned nineteen, and even though her faith hadn't managed to make a convert out of him, he'd seen and heard enough to know that there had to be *something* out there. He just didn't know what. But, boy oh boy, would Grandmom be filled with righteous indignation if she knew he'd married a Russian atheist!

The restaurant they were in was magnificent, and if it weren't for the view behind them, they could easily forget they were actually floating in the middle of the ocean. The waiter came over to their table.

"Are you lovely people ready to order?" he asked with an accent Jack didn't recognize.

"Give us a few more seconds," he answered.

"Certainly, sir." He glided away.

Jack reached his hands out across the table and took Stacey's hands in his, looking her straight in the eye. "I love you so much."

"I love you, too." She leaned forward across the table and kissed him passionately, gliding her tongue over his lips as she withdrew. "Order me something strong."

AFTER DINNER, DANCING, AND bowling, they were both relatively drunk and couldn't keep from laughing as they walked to the elevator en route to the night's top performance on the main stage. Descending, the glass walls of the elevator gave them a bird's-eye view of the ship's atrium area. It resembled a shopping mall with its kiosks, escalators, and fountains. There was even a grand piano being played.

"I haven't gotten this drunk since Joseph was conceived," Stacey exclaimed, leaning on Jack and finding his back pocket.

"What are you talking about?" He laughed. "You were as sober as a judge..." He cracked up at the old saying.

"That must've been the other guy, then!" She hit him in the chest, laughing louder.

The elevator reached the floor, and they stumbled out. "Which way to the stage, please?" Jack called out, feigning seriousness while crossing his arms and pointing in opposite directions.

A woman standing behind a semicircular counter that was actually a fish tank pointed them toward the front of the ship.

Jack waved his thanks and then looked to Stacey, horrified. "Hey," he whispered, "you see that?"

"What?"

"That lady's standing in the fish tank."

"I think she's standing behind it, babe."

He stood back and pondered this revelation. "Oh. Well, should we throw her a life preserver just in case?"

"She'll be fine! Now, go!" She shoved him in the back.

"Okay, okay..."

They sat at a round table in the back of the room so that they could continue frequenting the bar. It wasn't like they needed to be in the front row, throwing their undergarments at the feet of this Bob Marley cover band anyway—though had they been closer, anything would've been possible.

"Another drink?" she asked him once the music started pumping and the lights started strobing.

He nodded, and as she walked to the bar, he studied her. The dress didn't cover her back, and the giant disco ball hanging over the stage sent the laser show that accompanied the act dancing across her bare skin. He couldn't wait to get back to their room.

Then the alcohol pierced a hole through his defense system, and those forbidden thoughts began leaking through one drop at a time. He thought of what life would be like without her. Of what Joseph's life would be like without her.

A tear slid down his face.

No. It wouldn't happen. They wouldn't let it. They would beat this disease if it cost them every cent they would ever make. He shook the thought from his head, plugging the hole and refortifying his resolve to forget, for two weeks, that this thing called cancer even existed.

Stacey came walking back to him like a fantasy walking through a dream, the music playing, her soundtrack, the rays of light glorifying her essence. She sat in his lap. After taking a sip of whatever she'd ordered, she grabbed the back of his head and pressed her mouth against his.

He moved his hands across her back, cherishing the feel of her skin beneath his fingertips.

5

HE PRACTICALLY TORE HER dress off once they got back to the suite, and what started in the doorway ended out on the balcony, neither one of them in their drunken state conscious of how loud they'd been.

Jack stepped out of the shower, which he'd taken to wash some of the stupor away, and stepped into the bedroom. Lying on her side across the bed was Stacey in a black lace piece of lingerie he'd never seen before. She gave him a daring smile as he let the towel slip away. This was going to be the best two weeks ever.

EXHAUSTED, JACK COLLAPSED ONTO the bed.

"I love you," he whispered.

"I love you," Stacey responded. She didn't seem as drunk all of a sudden. She got up from the bed and slipped out of what she'd somehow managed to keep on during the last half hour. "I'm going to walk down to the internet café."

He rolled onto his back. "Why?"

"I want to see how Joseph is doing."

Jack chuckled. "Your mom probably has him halfway to Russia by now." When she didn't respond, he rolled to his side and found her standing there in the shadows, naked and staring at him. There was a strange expression on her face, one that he couldn't place but that seemed to embody a general sadness. Maybe regret. "What?"

"Nothing." She pulled on a pair of jeans and walked to the door. "I'll be right back."

"First of all, you're topless. Second of all, why don't you just call on your cell?" She looked down at her breasts as if examining them or consulting them. It was an unpleasant thought that she might have to lose them. He wondered if that was what she was thinking.

When she finally looked up, she smiled. But it was a forced smile. "That would have turned some heads." She went for a shirt. "The phone doesn't have a signal. Don't worry about it. I'll be right back. It's only two decks down."

"Okay, but be careful. Remember that *60 Minutes* episode."

"Yeah, yeah... I'll be back."

He tried not thinking of Arnold Schwarzenegger making the statement as the door closed. Instead, he wanted to play back the night a few times. But then his mind went crazy, and scenes from Arnold's *Red Heat* began playing through his head—the movie in which he played a Russian cop. It wasn't what he wanted to be thinking about. But then he noticed Stacey's phone lighting up on the bedside table. *That figures*, he thought. He saw a text message from a number that wasn't in her address book—no name, profile, or prior history accompanying it. The message didn't make any sense, though, just random numbers. *Must be a wrong number...* He slid into a madhouse of clouded dreams.

When he next opened his eyes, it was because of a mounting pressure building on his chest and a sensation in his groin.

"Hey, baby." Stacey's voice fluttered through his drunken sleep. He forced his eyes open, and after they adjusted a little, he saw her sitting on top of him. Though there were no lights on in the room, the moon was hanging full out over the ocean and shining down on their bed. Stacey's naked body was outlined by its silver hue.

THIS TIME, JACK WOKE up slightly annoyed. He had been in a deep sleep and enjoying a pleasant dream that he really wanted to get to the end of. He opened his eyes, expecting to see his wife's full, cancer-ridden breasts swaying over him.

But he saw nothing.

He turned to his right and saw that Stacey's spot was empty. Perhaps it was her getting out of bed that woke him? He started to lift himself to his elbows when something suddenly clasped over his mouth and pushed his head back down into the pillow.

What the—Stacey had never brought anything like that to their bed before.

He could just make out her hovering form, her hand clamped tightly over his mouth. Then he realized that she was wearing a glove, its cold leathery feel slipping between his lips. He wondered where she could've gotten a glove.

He reached out and grabbed her shoulders.

But they were not the shoulders of a slender woman.

Just as he started to struggle against the hand holding his head down, more hands materialized and grabbed his wrists, pinning them to the bed beside him. Then came the distinct sound of duct tape being pulled away from its roll. The gloved hand came off his face just long enough for the tape to be smashed against his mouth.

As the invisible hands lifted him off the bed, the moonlight washed over the forms surrounding him. There were three of them, all in black, masks covering their faces.

The balcony door slid open on its track, and he was carried, flailing like a fish in their strong hands, out into the night air.

No.

He felt the railing collide with his body.

No!

Then his feet were up off the deck, the railing beneath him.

NO!

And he was falling.

STACEY!

He was half-convinced that he was dreaming, that the Koontz novel he was reading had sunk into his subconscious and laid down roots.

Until he hit the water.

The millisecond of cognition that lingered after the strike allowed a final, timeless string of thoughts to go speeding through his head. It started with Stacey, evolved to Joseph, and then ended with an uncertain fear as to what was next. He didn't know what scared him more, his wife's atheism that promised the eternal nothingness of nonexistence, or the possibility of his own agnosticism's endless suffering.

Perhaps he should have considered it sooner.

6

HIS EYES SNAPPED OPEN, and a flood of icy water filled his lungs. He needed to breathe, to cough. He looked up, saw the light of the moon reaching through the black waters above him, and started moving his arms and legs. They felt as if they were encased in concrete, the cold water and the shock of the impact immobilizing him. Slowly, each kick of his legs a solitary act of will, he began moving closer to the shimmering light.

With an explosion, he broke through the choppy surface, ripped the tape from his mouth, and inhaled the night air in one desperate gulp. He was alive. He didn't know how, but he was alive. Though their suite wasn't located on one of the top decks, it was still a fall that should have killed him.

But that consolation quickly faded into the invisible horizon, along with the floating city and all its lights.

No.

Panic began swarming around his beating heart, squeezing it with a relentless embrace. This couldn't be happening. Had to be a dream.

He kicked his legs, trying to keep his head above the waves slapping his face. As he turned to look behind him, he imagined the red dot charting their progress on the television. That was hours ago. Florida would be over a hundred miles behind them by now.

He started swimming after the boat, not caring how futile it was. He refused to die without a fight—even a meaningless one.

He started crying, the ship growing smaller and smaller, the nothingness around him pressing in. "Oh, please, God... Oh, please, God..." He repeated it over and over again, swimming naked through what would soon be his grave.

He spun onto his back and stared up at the moonlit sky. And once again, nature's majesty was there to mock all the insignificant things man held dear.

Money, status, power... It was all nothing in the grand scheme of the cosmos. Nothing really mattered. Nothing but love, for it was only love that made him cry out against the moon's static presence. It wasn't power or all the trinkets he was about to lose that had him screaming at the top of his lungs. It was Stacey. And Joseph.

"HELP!" he shouted. "*HELP!*"

How could this be happening? It didn't make any sense. How could it all end this way? Why? "*HELP ME!*"

The sound of the expanse surrounding him stretched into liquid eternity, formless fingers snapping and spraying the night sky with a salty mist.

His arms were growing tired, his muscles burning, his heart racing. The boat continued to fade away, leaving him behind.

Oh, Jesus...

He was in such a state of shock that the full gravity of his situation had yet to dawn on him. It was there, knocking on his soul, trying to be comprehended, but Jack refused to give in, refused to believe that this was real. It couldn't be real. He couldn't die like this. All alone in the middle of the ocean. He needed to see Stacey, to tell her it would be okay. He needed to hold Joseph one more time and tell him how much he loved him. No, he wasn't ready to die!

He wondered how long it would take. How long could he stay afloat? An hour? Two? What about sharks? But within seconds, his torment at not being able to properly say goodbye to his family transferred to thoughts of what was to come. The afterlife. Being faced with it so clearly now was terrifying. What if he had been wrong? What if Grandmom was right and there was a way he could've ensured a happy reunion with his family one day? Was it too late?

Suddenly, a dozen rays of light blinked into existence and began sweeping the waters around the boat, their long beams piercing the night air and spotlighting the water. Were they looking for him?

Oh, please...please...please...

As he watched the behemoth cut a wide arc through the dark sea, his panic began to rise once more. That he would drown just as the ship was coming into range or that a shark would grab him for a nighttime snack just as salvation was extending its hand to him seemed like something the Fates might get a kick out of. He thought of Stacey's dream, the alligators chewing on them...

He stopped swimming, hoping to conserve his energy. He needed to stay afloat as long as possible. The search had begun rather quickly, so someone must have seen him fall into the water.

Or perhaps they were looking for someone else.

Stacey.

And then, spitting another mouthful of saltwater from his mouth, he wondered if he actually *should* survive. Cancer would be a long battle, but at least there was the possibility of victory. If he was pulled from the water only to be informed that his wife had also gone overboard... Death might be easier than facing that, assuming that what came next wasn't what Father Jacob had warned about all those years ago. But eternity was a long time to be wrong about something. Besides, he didn't *know* what had happened to Stacey, and as heart-shattering as it would be to confront Joseph, there was no way he could abandon him to Viktoriya. He'd promised Joseph that he would never leave him, so he would do whatever he could to make it true. That meant ignoring the burning fire spreading into his shoulders and the cramping in his legs.

Come on. You can do it. For Stacey. For Joseph. Oh, sweet Jesus, please...

The lights came within range just as Jack was sure he was finished. Summoning some inner strength he didn't know existed, he used the last of his energy to splash and scream. He was only a shadow on the dark waves, and a light swept over him half a dozen more times without the bells and whistles he'd expect to accompany a discovery. He was having trouble keeping his head above the water now, and he could feel the will to survive begin to slip away. The mysterious deep lingering below his cramping legs summoned him.

Just as his head slipped beneath the ocean, he thought he heard a small outboard motor whining above the wind.

7

EVERYTHING WAS A BLUR. Hands grabbing him, pulling him. Voices spilling down from a collage of rotating faces letting him know he was on his back. He could make out first aid equipment whenever one of the faces moved from his line of sight, and he knew he was in the ship's infirmary. But all he could think of was Stacey.

He forced himself to a sitting position, the room and its faces spinning.

"Sir, what is your name?" It came as a chorus of echoes.

"Green," he muttered.

One of the men spun and motioned to someone behind him, who then flew out of the room.

"Mr. Green, are you okay? Can you tell us what happened?"

"Stacey..." he whispered.

"Who is Stacey, Mr. Green?"

"Stacey..."

"Mr. Green, how did you fall off the ship?"

His eyes were locked on nothing, a spell cast by the trauma he couldn't escape. "They had masks on..."

"Who had masks on?"

"Stacey..."

"Stacey had a mask on?" The man looked confused.

No, you idiot. Not Stacey! Why would Stacey have a mask on?

"Mr. Green, we need to know if you were alone. Do you remember what room you're in?"

At that moment, the man who had run out of the room popped his head back in. "Jack and Stacey Green. The Eden suite."

"Eden..." A dozen scenarios could be seen playing out behind the man's eyes. "Mr. Green," he said, trying to get him to focus, "did you fall from your balcony?"

But he could only whisper, "Masks..."

The man stood and began directing traffic. "Take care of him. Let me know when he becomes lucid. You check the room. Everyone else, start searching for

Mrs. Green. Get photocopies of her ID and start handing them out. Do it quietly, but do it quickly and efficiently. We've been through this. You know what to do."

The crowd in the room dispersed.

"You're lucky someone saw you hit the water, Mr. Green. And that they raised an alarm."

8

ONCE JACK REGAINED HIS senses, everything came back to him at once. "Stacey!" He jumped to his feet, and the infirmary staff, along with a security guard, moved to restrain him.

"Where's my wife?" Jack screamed, trying to push past them.

"Mr. Green, please sit down and relax!"

"Where's my wife? Get off me!"

"Sir, please..."

Jack punched him in the throat.

More hands came at him, but he swatted them away and broke into the hallway. Hearing radios crackle behind him, he ran to the closest wall map, the YOU ARE HERE marker on the diagram letting him know how to get back to their suite. He took off sprinting down the carpeted hallway, cabin doors racing by him in blurs. When he came to the steps, he took them two at a time until he reached the appropriate deck. He didn't know what time it was, but the fact that the ship was nearly deserted told him it was early. He flew past a row of duty-free shops and through a café before rounding the corner to the suites.

Crew members and security personnel were congregated in the hallway by his door.

"Stacey!" He pushed himself through them and stumbled into the room, only to be apprehended by two giant men.

"Where is she?" he hollered, and tears leaked down his face.

"Sir, we need you to calm down," stated one of the men holding him.

Your wife's missing on a boat that's floating in the middle of the ocean, and you were thrown overboard by men in black ski masks... Please just calm down.

"Tell us what happened." He recognized the voice from the infirmary.

"I woke up and three masked men were in here. They grabbed me and took me out to the balcony." He was talking loud and fast, thinking that time was short, thinking that Stacey might be out in the water somewhere.

"They threw you over?"

He aimed a furious stare at the man. "No, I *asked* them if they could assist me with a swim."

"We're just trying to help, Mr. Green."

"By sitting around in my suite? My wife could be..." Anger began giving way to hopelessness. "She could be... Oh, God..." He was motioning toward the balcony, and the tears suddenly came unimpeded. "You have to search the water."

"We did, Mr. Green."

His breath caught. "What do you mean you *did*?"

"That was almost three hours ago, sir. I know you understand."

Three *hours*? How had that much time —wait. "Understand what?" He craned his neck, trying to get a glimpse of the guy holding him. But the strong arms didn't relent and neither did any information.

The man doing all the talking took a deep breath and seemed about to walk out of the room.

"Where the hell are you going?" he screamed. "Get back here and answer my questions!"

Turning with deliberate poise, the man set his gaze on him. "*If* your wife went overboard, sir, and *if* she survived the fall, there is no way she could tread that water for three hours. I'm sorry, but we've resumed our normal heading."

"You *what*?" And he thought of Stacey in the water, watching the ship fade away as he had. He struggled against the monster restraining him, flailing wildly until he was completely spent. The man then dropped him to the floor. Crumpling to his knees, Jack attempted to get a grip on himself. He didn't *know* that Stacey went overboard. He didn't *know* that she was...

His hands were shaking, his eyes wide with incomprehension.

"Get him some clothes," he heard someone say. He looked down at himself. He was still naked. Under any other circumstance, he would be embarrassed. Right now, however, he couldn't bring himself to care at all.

"You left me naked for three hours?" he seethed.

A pair of pants was tossed to him, his own from one of the dressers. "Put these on, will you?"

Once he had his pants on, the man with all the good news said, "Mr. Green, I'm Doug Bennington, head of security on this ship. We're going to do everything we can to find out what happened to you and to locate your wife. But first, I need you to do a few things. One, appreciate the miracle of your being alive right now. Two, stop assaulting my men. And three"—he handed him a note —"explain *this* to me."

Jack took the note from him and tried to calm down as the words danced in his trembling grasp. Finally, he looked up to Bennington. "Where did you find this?"

"It was on the bedside table. You didn't write it?"

He shook his head.

"Is it your wife's handwriting?"

He stumbled for some kind of meaning or explanation, but nothing came. It didn't make sense. "I think so."

Bennington sighed. "Are you still sticking with your masked men story?"

"What?" Jack's eyes snapped upward. "What the hell do you think? You think I'm making it up? That we... You think *I*..." But he couldn't bring himself to say it.

"I know only three things. We fished you out of the water, your wife is missing, and there's a suicide note that she supposedly wrote. How do *you* think it looks, Mr. Green?"

He didn't say anything. What could he say? His mind was too busy swimming against the whirlpool of disaster for any kind of rational response.

"Well," Bennington said, "I'm afraid we're going to have to confine you to your room for the duration of the trip."

A COUPLE OF HOURS later, Jack was alone, sitting on the bed. He was running every detail he could recall over and over inside his spinning head, but they were all insignificant and offered no clue as to why masked men would want him and Stacey dead. He thought of Joseph, his little blond-haired buddy, and missed him more than he ever thought possible. But how could he return home without Stacey? How could he survive his son's reaction to *that* news? He had to find her.

There was a knock on the door before the *beep* of an electronic card unlocked it. Bennington stepped in.

"Anything?" Jack asked, barely able to lift his head.

"We're still looking."

Jack thrust a hand through his hair. "So what happens now? Besides holding me prisoner?"

"It will be handled by the police force once we reach port."

"What police force? You'd better mean the FBI, pal."

"The country that holds the ship's registration is responsible for handling these matters."

"Excuse me?"

"I understand your frustration, but that's the way things are," Bennington explained.

Jack leaned forward, his eyes on fire. "You're telling me that since the ship is registered in the Bahamas, it's up to the Bahama police to investigate what happened to my wife?"

"That is correct."

Standing, Jack began to pace, his blood boiling. "I can't believe this," he muttered under his breath.

"You're a US citizen, so there is a good chance the FBI will get involved."

"You don't believe me, do you? You actually think that I tossed my wife off the ship."

Bennington sighed. "Including staff, there are almost six thousand people on this ship whom we are still responsible for. We have a suicide note written by your missing wife—"

"And you have my testimony that three men threw me off the boat!"

"There's nothing more we can do, Mr. Green. I really am very sorry. We'll continue to search the ship, but until we reach port and allow the proper authorities to take over, all we can do is hope she's okay."

"Hope she's okay?" Hot tears were suddenly streaking down his face. "Do I look like someone who wants to die? Like someone who came out here to jump? Like some lunatic who wanted to get rid of his wife?" The resolve he'd spent building over the last two hours slowly melted away beneath a whole new wave of grief. "She had cancer! We came here for one last good time before..." He clenched his fists. "Why would she jump the first night?" He sobbed in frustration, wanting to feel the guy's vertebrae crackle and pop in his bare hands. "And you think I'm making up the masked men? For what reason?"

Bennington stood and calmly shrugged. "I don't know you, so I obviously can't answer that question. Maybe you forced her to write the letter, and then you threw her overboard, except that you slipped yourself. Or maybe you wrote the letter."

Jack almost charged the man.

"All I'm saying is that I'm ill-equipped to do anything more in this situation. It's a matter for the police now. As soon as we reach port, the proper authorities will be here to further investigate. In the meantime, I have six thousand other passengers to look after."

9

JACK SPENT THE NEXT two days sitting on a bed and staring at a blank hotel wall in Nassau while the local police force did as little investigating into his wife's disappearance and his own "alleged" abduction as possible. He would have taken a flight home sooner had he not been so terrified of confronting Joseph with the news of his mother's death. It was news he had once gotten himself, and he couldn't stomach the thought of introducing such pain to his son now. Every time he picked up the phone to call a taxi, he imagined Joseph's face reacting to such a world-altering report. Even now, after so many years, Jack's own heart still bore the scars of such news. After slamming the phone back into its cradle, he could only bury his head in his hands and start sobbing all over again.

Today was different though.

Now, day three of this nightmare, he yearned desperately to hear Joseph's voice, to see his smile. He needed his son if he was going to make it another week, needed to hear his voice if he was going to make it another day. The knowledge that they would eventually get through this, but that they would need each other in order to do so, seemed like the only thing anchoring Jack to a rock that was spiraling crazily through the galaxy. If not for his son, he would be spending the next week and a half getting as drunk as possible in preparation for the trip back to Miami—with, of course, no intention of actually reaching Miami. Without Stacey his life would be a joke, the punch line not worth sticking around for.

So Joseph would have to fill that hole, become the sun that rose over his world every morning, the only star capable of blotting out the pain. But he needed to hear his son's squeaky voice now, before the grief stormed back and changed his mind.

He swore, slammed the phone, and then slammed it down again for added measure. Joseph and Mother Viktoriya were failing to answer his calls. He stared at it, his mind racing through different scenarios that might prevent them from picking up the phone. There were limitless possibilities, most of which were innocent enough. Still, he felt a bubble of concern rising in his stomach. He grabbed the phone and called a taxi.

After arrangements were made, he walked to the bed and picked up their luggage—his and Stacey's—before leaving the hotel room. It was time to go home. He was done waiting for the police. It was obvious, no matter how much pressure he put on them, that nothing was going to be done. And though he hated to admit it, now that they were docked, there was probably nothing they could do. Even if they did believe him, the men in masks were surely gone by now. With no body of evidence, nothing but his word and that suicide note...

The suicide note.

It chipped at his subconscious, an itch begging to be scratched. But there was still too much shock and pain for a clear evaluation of all the facts. That was all for another time. Now he just needed to get on a plane and figure out how he was going to explain this to his son.

10

HE COULDN'T TAKE HIS eyes off the water below. An image of Stacey bobbing up and down somewhere out there would not leave him. And the empty seat beside him just laughed, taunting his inability to process the sudden, horrifying turn of events.

When he finally managed to peel his eyes off the ocean, he wondered again if leaving Nassau translated into giving up on Stacey. What if she wasn't floating facedown but had been kidnapped and was actually alive on the islands he'd just left? But even if that were the case, what could he do about it? He wasn't familiar with the Bahamas, didn't know a single person who could help him. He wasn't one of the characters in a movie who always seemed to have the necessary background needed to go on a solo rescue mission—as if this sort of thing only happened to ex-intelligence officers or army veterans. He was a salesman from Philadelphia. Any chance he'd have at finding his wife would come via the FBI or Interpol or some agency that knew how to find US citizens abroad. Because he sure as hell didn't.

"Excuse me, sir, can I get you anything?" a stewardess asked, leaning over.

He rolled his heavy eyes to the young lady. "Something strong...please."

"Would you like—"

"Anything. The strongest you have." He leaned forward and lowered his voice. "And as much as you can."

"Sir, I—"

"Listen, Kati," he said, his eyes focusing on her nametag, "my wife is somewhere out there...floating." He threw a thumb over his shoulder at the window.

Her brow furrowed.

"We were on a cruise," he said, and his voice matched the flatness in his eyes.

Her hand went to her mouth as if the surprise might physically leap out of it. "Oh, I am so sorry, sir... I..."

He nodded. "Something strong. Please."

TWO HOURS LATER, HE was pretty well drunk. But in his drunkenness, the anguish that had for three days prevented any kind of analytical process receded just enough. He reached into the seatback in front of him and extracted a magazine. He opened it up to the emptiest page he could find and started making notes.

—*men in black masks*

—*suicide note*

But that was as far as he could get. There were no other pieces to include. So, emerging from the depths of drunken stupor was the conclusion that the whole thing must have been a case of mistaken identity. It was the only thing that made sense. Someone got a room number mixed up. *Drugs...* They'd mistaken him for some dealer who crossed his supplier. Had to be. But then what would they do with Stacey...*to* Stacey? He didn't want to think about that now, not while his brain was actually emotionally numb enough to process the thought.

He leaned back against the headrest and massaged his temples. *Think.* When he got home, he would contact the FBI himself. The police in the Bahamas, along with the security people from the boat, assured him that they had reported the incident to the FBI, but he didn't necessarily believe that. Their whole approach had been to do nothing at all, choosing to disbelieve his story rather than to do anything worthwhile about it. So as soon as he could, he would get on a computer and search for more options, see who had jurisdiction and who might be able to help.

As soon as I can...

The guy sitting in front of him was sound asleep, his laptop open on the empty seat beside him.

Beyond the point of caring, Jack reached around the seat and quietly took the man's computer. After taking another reassuring peek at the man's tanned eyelids, he placed a finger on the touchpad and brought the screen to life. Thankfully, there was a portable Wi-Fi device plugged into one of the USB ports, and the computer was already logged onto the internet. The man's Facebook status was up, and judging from the pictures he'd just uploaded, his time in the Bahamas had been a little on the wild side. Jack minimized the page and opened a new one.

Half an hour later, the man still asleep in front of him, he had found enough information on cruise ship crime to infuriate him all over again. In his searching for some kind of direction, he'd come across a dozen sites dedicated to cruise victims. Hundreds of stories were documented. Drug trafficking, rape, theft, missing children, murder… The accounts of negligence, cover-ups, and lies by the cruise lines in these instances were maddening, provoking one congressman to declare there being no better place to commit a crime than on a cruise ship. You were almost guaranteed to get away with it.

In one instance that Jack read about, a woman had gone missing—the crew packing away her possessions and failing to inform anyone that she'd even disappeared! The police were never contacted nor was her family. Not until her father reported her missing had anything been done. And even then it took the cruise ship company three days to even confirm that she'd been a passenger on the ship!

The number of disappearances over the years was staggering, from little children to crew members. One report he saw estimated that a person went overboard every two weeks.

Had Jack known all this, he wouldn't have been so eager to accept Viktoriya's offer.

But he found the most disturbing part to be how commonplace it seemed for the incidents to be swept under the rug. One case involved a naked woman found drugged and dead in a room with four men…and no conviction.

The man began to move, and Jack quickly closed out his window and maximized the Facebook page. He reached around the chair and placed the laptop back on the seat while the man rubbed his eyes, looking out the window.

Yeah, Jack thought as he waved down the stewardess for another drink, he would call the FBI as soon as he got home. He was sure now that absolutely nothing had been done to find either his wife or the men who had thrown them overboard.

And there was going to be hell to pay for it.

11

THE EMPTY SILENCE COMING from the Sonata's vacant seat beside him was even more haunting than what he'd endured on the plane. He was driving their car, approaching their house. But there was no "their" anymore—as the empty seat proclaimed. It was just "his" now. And in the quiet, he could hear Stacey's faint screams as she sank beneath the eerie darkness and reached out for the same moonlit sky he'd reached for. Only there had been no one there to answer her cries.

Tears failed to exorcise the emotion, and the repeated blows to the steering wheel only hurt his hands. What was he going to say to Joseph? How were they going to get past this? And why couldn't he get a hold of Viktoriya?

The dotted lines of I-95 continued coming at him, northeast Philly along with the next chapter of his life growing nearer. It was a chapter he wanted to curse the author for, though not while still hoping for His help.

About ten miles from the house, an internal numbness started taking over, chasing unstable feelings from the pilot's chair and establishing a cold stoicism in its place. It was a mutiny that he knew wouldn't last long, but for now the ability to not feel was a welcome one.

He turned down their street, and their house came into view. The driveway was empty. He frowned, wondering where his mother-in-law and son could be. But then maybe not having to deliver the news now would buy him more time to wake up.

Daddy, where's Mommy?

Come here, buddy. There's something I have to tell you...

As he pulled into the driveway, he decided he'd call the FBI while waiting for Joseph to get back from wherever the countess had taken him. His friend Donny was a Philadelphia cop. He could put him in contact with the FBI.

He struggled with their bags as he attempted to slip the key into the front door. But when his bag slipped off his shoulder and swung into it, the door swung open. *Are you kidding me?* How many times had he reminded Viki to keep all the doors locked? He crossed the threshold and stepped into a house that he knew would never feel the same again.

When he entered their bedroom, he was instantly bombarded with an endless parade of memories and the familiar feel of Stacey's presence. For a second, everything seemed normal, that it *had* all been a bad dream. He half-expected her to walk out of the bathroom wearing a teasing smile and the pink lingerie they'd discussed before leaving for the airport. As if everything between now and then had been a split-second imagining and Viktoriya was still on her way, the ship not boarded. But she didn't step out of the bathroom this time. Because she was floating somewhere in the middle of the Atlantic, bloated and nibbled by fish.

He took out his cell phone and dialed Donny. As the ringing sounded in his ear, he sat down on the bed that he'd shared with Stacey for five years, wondering where this twisted road would lead him.

SIX HOURS LATER, THE sun now beginning to set over the homes across the street, Joseph still hadn't shown up with Mother Russia. Maybe she'd taken him to Sesame Place for the day. Or maybe she'd finally decided to "run away." He smiled at the thought, remembering the last conversation he'd had with Joseph.

That's silly, Daddy. Grandma can't run. She's too old...

Sudden movement outside the kitchen window kicked his heart into a pit. He took a deep breath. The time had come to destroy his son's sense of innocence...of justice and fairness, to turn everything he knew about the world upside down. The news, like a switch thrown on one of life's twisted tracks, would send the four-year-old swerving off in a different direction and away from the balanced structure meant to stabilize him. Without a "faithful" Grandmom to rebuild his life, as Jack had had in the wake of his disaster, Joseph's world would become one of pain, confusion, and uncertainty.

But it wasn't Viktoriya's big Buick pulling into the driveway, just his neighbor taking out some trash.

Jack stepped out the side door and walked to the chain-link fence separating his property from the next. "Hey, Steve," he said over the fence.

Steve looked up from the trashcan he'd just dropped some bags in, and surprise settled on his face. "Oh, hi, Jack... What are you... I thought you were gone until next week?"

He shrugged. "Yeah, well..." He had no desire to talk about this now. "Hey, have you seen my mother-in-law or Joseph? They're not here, and I can't reach them on the cell."

Steve stepped away from the trash can and leaned against the fence. Using a middle finger to push heavy glasses back up his nose, he said, "Yeah, they left two days ago."

"What do you mean?"

"They loaded up the car and took off. I watched them from the window. Joseph waved to me." He smiled. "That's a good kid you got there, Jack."

"Where was she taking him?"

"I don't know. She didn't tell you guys that she was taking him?"

"No."

"Huh." A shadow of concern settled over his face. "They packed quite a bit, like they were gonna be gone for a week or so. I just figured she was taking him to some resort or something while you were away."

"She left the front door open," Jack muttered.

"And you can't reach her on the phone?"

Jack squinted at his house, wondering what Viktoriya was doing and how Joseph might be interpreting it. *That's silly, Daddy. Grandma can't run. She's too old.* "No," he answered softly.

"That's weird." Steve stepped back from the fence and brushed a hand through his graying hair. "I'm sure they're okay, though." But what else was he going to say?

And then Jack thought of something. *Maybe she did tell someone*. "Thanks, Steve." He retreated inside, leaving his neighbor stranded in mid-thought.

Steve peered over the fence. "Glad you're back," he called out after him. "I think..."

Jack took the stairs to the second floor two at a time. He thought that maybe Viktoriya left a message for them that he'd missed, but first he wanted to check Joseph's room. After opening some of the red and white drawers with the Phillies' logo between the handles, he noticed that, indeed, most of Joseph's clothes were gone. As were his favorite stuffed animals and toys. Jack stood there in the middle of the room and tried his hardest to keep it from spinning. *What is happening?*

When no immediate reply came to him, he went into his bedroom and to Stacey's luggage. It was still sitting on the floor at the foot of their bed. *Their* bed. He grabbed the duffel bag, unzipped it, and flipped it upside down, emptying its contents onto the covers. He was looking for her cell phone. Maybe, just maybe, Viktoriya had left a voicemail for her.

But the phone wasn't there.

Why wouldn't her phone be here? She had been as naked as he was when the men had come into their suite, and he knew that he hadn't missed it when gathering her stuff to leave. Actually, he thought, he couldn't really be certain that she'd been in the room when they came in. She could've gone for a walk. Unlikely? Yes. But in a court of law, there was no way he could prove that she was there in the room with him at that time.

The doorbell rang.

His heart leaped. But then Viktoriya wouldn't be ringing the doorbell, would she?

He relaxed. There was a mirror on the dresser across from him. He stared at it, focused on his reflection. It wasn't one of the better portraits the mirror had painted of him, and he wondered what must be going through Steve's mind right now. His jaw was covered in black stubble, his hair greasy and unkempt. The clothes that he was wearing, he'd been wearing for days, and there was now a sweet, bitter odor clinging to them. He moved his gaze to his own eyes, staring deep, and didn't like what he saw there at all. It was a look that Joseph could never see.

He left the bedroom and, without caring to make himself any more presentable, descended the stairs to a *ding-dong* soundtrack. He pulled open the big wooden door, peered through the screening of the next, and saw a silhouette of what he figured to be a man, the sun descending just behind him.

Jack shielded his eyes against the glare. "Can I help you?"

"Special Agent Johnson with the FBI. Are you Mr. Green?"

"Yeah."

"We have a mutual friend. Donny Rickards. He called me a little while ago, told me what happened. I'm very sorry."

Jack nodded, a bowling ball lodged in his throat. He wiped a tear away with the back of his hand. The icy stoicism was beginning to melt.

"I'd like to see if I can help. If you'd like that," Agent Johnson said.

"Yeah, yeah, of course. Thanks." He pushed the door open and stepped to the side, gesturing for the FBI man to enter.

As Jack led him to the living room, he noticed the agent eyeballing his book collection and wondered if he might be in handcuffs by the end of the visit. *Jerry...* The sudden thought of never hearing that name come from Stacey's lips again sent another fissure racing across his thawing resolve.

Agent Johnson must've noticed. "You okay?"

"Yeah," he muttered. "You want anything to drink?"

"I'm fine, thank you."

They settled into sofas, each facing the other.

FBI was sweeping the room with his eyes, taking in photographs, pictures, and unfortunately, his burned DVD collection from Ivan.

"It's a free country," Jack stated.

Agent Johnson set his dark, expressionless eyes on him and allowed a small grin to stretch his lips.

"Well," Jack tried clarifying, "it's supposed to be, in theory. I mean, we say it is, but—"

Johnson frowned.

"I mean—"

"Mr. Green," he interrupted, a softness settling over his demeanor, "I'm here about your missing wife."

Jack brought a hand up to his mouth and averted his glassy eyes, shaking his head. It was so hard to talk about. To face it. As long as it was trapped in his head, it could be the product of a dream, a misunderstanding...but to lay it out in words with other people would make it real. Thank God Joseph wasn't here now with the FBI in the house; that would've been a mess.

"Tell me what happened."

The man's size was intimidating, but there was a gentleness that rounded out the edges of his federal persona. And though his suit and tie were stereotypical of the profession, Jack thought it made him look like a salesman. If not for the government-issued pistol strapped to his waist. If salesmen carried guns, Jack mused, he would be living in a much bigger house.

"Call me paranoid, but do you think I can see some ID first?"

Johnson smiled reassuringly and reached into his jacket. He pulled it out, flipping it open in classic fashion, his picture and the three blue letters beside it authenticating him.

"Do you guys practice doing that?"

"Sometimes."

He sighed and sat back. "I don't know what happened." He brought his hand up to his mouth. "We were drunk, having a good time. She was *really* drunk." He smiled sadly, recalling their carelessness. "We ate dinner, danced, went to a show..."

"And then?"

"We went back to the suite."

"What time was that?"

"I have no idea. Close to midnight."

"And you fell asleep?" Agent Johnson leaned forward.

"Yeah, we fell asleep, and then..." He frowned.

"What?"

The timeline of events suddenly came back to him. "No, *I* went to sleep. She went to the internet café."

"At midnight?"

"This would've been after midnight now." Jack stared out the window and watched some pigeons sidestep in unison across the power lines, like some kind of line dance to a birdsong only they could hear. "She almost walked out of the room topless."

"She was still drunk?"

He nodded.

"Why did she need the internet at that particular time?"

"She said she wanted to see how Joseph was doing, said her cell wasn't getting a signal."

"Joseph is your son?"

"Yeah. He was staying here with my mother-in-law." He shook his head. "As soon as she left, she got a text message. Figures."

Johnson began working the inside of his lip. "And was that the last time you saw her?"

"No. She came back."

"You said you were asleep? How do you know—"

"She woke me up."

"For..."

"Yeah." If the admission of such passionate copulating made Johnson uncomfortable, he didn't show it.

"And what condition were you in at this point?"

"I was pretty out of it, I guess. It was dark, I was still drunk, and I'd just been woken out of a deep sleep."

A pause. Then Johnson asked, "Are you sure it was your wife?"

Jack looked at the man. "Of course I'm sure it was my wife." But he had to revisit the few images he could still bring up in his mind's eye to make sure. Yeah, it was her. "Why?" He couldn't pinpoint the true source of his questions.

"I don't know if I can help you or not, Mr. Green. But if there's any chance at all, I need to establish as many facts as I can. I don't know you. I don't know your wife. So the way I see it, the possibilities are limitless. I'm trying to eliminate certain scenarios just as much as I'm trying to establish others. Okay?"

Jack nodded.

"Okay, and then what?"

"Then we fell asleep."

"Your wife was right beside you?"

"Yeah."

"Okay, go on." He adjusted his tie.

He'd been so distressed over Stacey's disappearance that he hadn't really revisited the actual assault in any great detail. Doing so now sent a series of chills down his back. "Next thing I know, someone is sitting on my chest. I thought it was Stacey again, and I was starting to get annoyed. Then I noticed the hand covering my mouth had a glove on it, and by the time I realized it wasn't Stacey, I was being carried out of the room by three men."

"You saw them?"

"The moon was full and shining directly into our room. They were wearing masks."

"Did you see your wife at any point during this?"

Jack wagged his head. "No, she wasn't in the bedroom with them."

"How big was the suite? Could she have been in another room?"

"I guess so." He stood up. "Excuse me for a second." He left the room and closed himself in the hallway bathroom. Sitting on the toilet, he tried desperately to get a handle on himself. He could feel stuff unwinding and knew he was about to fall apart again. In one sense, talking about it was like relaying scenes from a movie he'd seen...an outlandish story comprised of fictional characters. Yet, on the other hand, talking about it was bringing back the terror that gripped his heart as he was falling overboard and screaming her name. Real and unreal, reality and dream, the two playing tug-of-war with his mind.

A knock on the bathroom door startled him, and he wiped his eyes.

"You okay, Mr. Green?" the agent asked.

Sniffling, Jack muttered, "Sure." He leaned over the sink and splashed some water on his face.

"The people in the masks, they threw you overboard?" Johnson asked from the other side of the door.

Jack wiped his face off with a towel. "Yeah."

"It's a miracle you survived."

Jack wasn't sure if the skepticism in his voice was imagined or not. When he opened the door, he answered, "Maybe."

"What do you mean?"

"Depends on how this all plays out, I guess." Of course it was the bitterness talking, the unfairness of having a loved one snatched away with no rhyme or reason as to why.

But Johnson wasn't about to psychoanalyze him, so he moved on to his next question. "Tell me about the note."

Jack walked back into the kitchen. "Security found a suicide note in our room. It looked like Stacey's writing."

"You think they forced her to write it?"

"Of course."

Johnson walked around the perimeter of the kitchen, silent.

"What?" Jack asked.

"Doesn't make sense."

"What doesn't?"

"That it was random."

Jack lowered his head, his hand pausing on the refrigerator handle. "I was thinking mistaken identity."

Johnson nodded his shaved head. "A hit meant for another couple in another room. Could be." He paused again. "Do you have the note?"

Jack opened the fridge and grabbed a beer. "Yeah. Security didn't even notice that I took it, and the police in Nassau never even asked to see it. You guys should really do something about that, the whole cruise thing, I mean. It's pathetic." Leaving the kitchen, he headed back up the steps. "I'll get it."

When he returned, he found Agent Johnson scrutinizing the framed photos that were lined up across the shelves of the entertainment center. "Here," he said, making his presence known.

Johnson turned and took the letter from him, taking a few seconds to read it over. When he finished, he looked up. "She had cancer?"

"Yeah, we'd just found out. That's why we were on the cruise, to get away for a couple of weeks before..." He trailed off, focusing on one of their wedding photos.

It seemed like a hundred years ago, yet the first day of their cruise had bridged the gap like only a time machine from some future world could. He tried not to imagine what the rest of the trip would have been like.

"Anyone else know that she had cancer?"

"Just her mother."

"That's it?"

"She didn't want to go through chemo. She was planning on pursuing other treatments and didn't want everyone's two cents about it."

"Kind of odd that she would want to make the note seem more authentic than she had to."

Jack's mouth was already open in response, but it ultimately fell shut without anything to say. *Why the hell would she mention the cancer?* The men wouldn't have known about it, so why make the note that much more convincing by revealing an unknown truth? And why would the men who had gone through the trouble of planning the thing even leave their cover story up to *her* imagination? None of it made sense. "Maybe she knew she was about to die, and this was her way of saying goodbye..." But it didn't seem like something Stacey would do. Not that he'd ever witnessed her in such a situation before.

"You think these men came into your suite, took your wife out of the bedroom, and then came back for you?"

The agent was right. There was no way that Stacey would have sat there next to the bed he was sleeping in while constructing a carefully concocted suicide note for three intruders who were going to kill her anyway. She would have screamed. Would have fought. No, if they threw her overboard, it had to have been after they tossed him, not before.

Johnson asked, "Do you have her cell phone? I'd like to see that text message she got."

"No. I don't know where it is. I was just looking for it myself, hoping her mother left a message letting her know where she took Joseph."

"You don't know where your son is?"

Jack raised his arms, defenseless against the question. "We weren't supposed to be back for another ten days. The neighbor saw them loading up her car with luggage the other day... I can't get a hold of them on the phone. I guess I'll drive over to her house after you leave. Maybe she just took him there."

Walking back to the mantel, Johnson touched the wedding photo Jack had been staring at. "How long have you been married?"

"Five years."

"How long did you know each other beforehand?"

"Not long at all, actually."

"What's your mother-in-law's name?" He left the picture.

"Viktoriya Arsov."

"Russian."

"Yeah."

The agent looked out the window. "She been here long?"

"In the northeast? As long as I've known her."

"Which hasn't been that long."

Jack was confused by this sudden string of questions. "I don't understand how that's relevant."

"Like I said, at this point I have no idea what is and isn't relevant. Do you mind if I pull your phone records, to see where that text came from?"

"No, I guess not."

"Email?"

The Jerry in him was starting to tingle. He glanced at his books and tried smiling. "Don't you think you're monitoring them already?"

"I doubt you made the cut," he quipped. "Go check your mother-in-law's house. In the meantime, I'll see if I can get the security tapes from the ship before they erase them."

"Thanks. I appreciate your help. I didn't know where else to go."

Johnson nodded his head toward the books, and Jack figured he'd had his eye on the one about the FBI setting up the 1993 World Trade Center bombing. But that was something that had been reported by the *New York Times* and Dan Rather and was a matter of public record now that the transcripts between Emad Salem and his FBI handlers were out of the bag. "Guess we're not all that bad after all," Johnson said.

Jack forced a humble smile. "No, not all of you." He walked him to the door.

Before stepping outside, Johnson looked him in the eyes. "Listen," he said. "I may be way out of line by saying this, but I think I'd want to hear it if I were in your shoes."

"What?"

"From everything you just told me, there is no actual evidence to suggest that your wife is dead."

That stunned him. "They searched the whole ship..."

"Security and the Nassau police? Doubt it."

Unbelief and a flare of hope simultaneously flickered in Jack's chest.

Recognizing it, Johnson held up his hand. "Don't go jumping for joy. I just don't want to see you do anything stupid. Also, you should be careful what you tell your son. Give me some time before you write her off, okay?" He handed him his business card. "You don't know anything yet."

All Jack could do was nod and accept the information.

After the FBI pulled away from his house, Jack closed the door and leaned his back against it. Sliding to a sitting position, he hugged his knees to his chest. He wept there for fifteen minutes, the arctic terrain inside melting away and returning to an emotional jungle full of life and pain. When he finally wiped the last tear from his eye, he got up and headed out the door. He was pretty certain that he wouldn't find Viktoriya or Joseph at her house, but he didn't know where else to look.

He made sure to lock the door behind him.

12

TWENTY-FIVE MINUTES LATER, THE sun was nowhere to be seen, and only the faint afterglow of twilight was left to illuminate the skies over Viktoriya's home. Jack pulled the Sonata into her driveway, the headlights reaching out in front of the car and sweeping over the small house before settling on the white garage doors at the top of the asphalt stretch. He turned the ignition off and got out of the car, studying the property for a few seconds. Nothing seemed out of place, but as he walked to the front, he knew that the house was entirely too dark for anyone awake to be there. He rang the doorbell.

No answer.

He skirted around the house, careful to avoid short rows of bushes and flowers before coming to the green chain-link fence separating the front yard from the back. Flipping the latch, he quickly went to the patio and tried the back door. *Figures she locks her own door.* He didn't know of any hidden key kept under a pot, but looking around, he saw that the patio was clear, not a single thing under which to hide a key. He wondered when she'd gotten rid of the outdoor furniture and the plastic flamingos. But peering through the window, not entirely unaware of how his behavior might appear to the neighbors, he was confronted by yet another mystery.

The living room was empty. And not empty as in no one was in it, but empty like...*empty*.

Throwing aside all reservation, he kicked the glass window above the doorknob, cracking the pane into big diagonal pieces that shattered when they hit the patio. There was nothing more recognizable than the sound of breaking glass, whether a bottle, a window, or a windshield, and any neighbor who heard the noise would ID it for sure. But he was beyond caring. Though an encounter with the police and the time it would take to explain things wouldn't help any.

Reaching through the broken glass, he unlocked the door from the other side. When he pulled the door open, more pieces of glass fell out of the window frame and exploded at his feet. A dog barked a few houses down.

"Viktoriya? Joseph?" he called out, stepping into the kitchen. It was completely empty, the cabinets all open and displaying nothing but vacant shelves. The humming of the refrigerator was the only indication of...anything. The stove wasn't plugged in, its digital clock blank. There were no other clocks, calendars, pictures, or measuring cups on the wall, no droplets of water trickling from the faucet beneath the now curtainless window. No trash can, coffee pot, microwave, toaster, paper towels, napkins, hand or dish soap. He opened the freezer. No ice cube trays. She was gone for sure. When the ice cube trays were missing, no one was coming back.

But the refrigerator was still running. Why unplug the stove and not the fridge? He knew that it was recommended the appliance be left plugged in up to three weeks even without use, so was she planning on returning? Or maybe unplugging the fridge just hadn't occurred to her. Or whoever she got to clear the place. It was obvious she hadn't moved herself out. After all, she was too old to even run.

He went to the sink and ran his finger underneath the faucet, feeling for any trace of water. It was dry. He turned both knobs on full and was rewarded with nothing. The water was shut off.

As he walked quickly through the rest of the house, worry finally began to set in. It was hard to avoid thinking that his mother-in-law's abandoned house was somehow related to the masked men on the cruise ship, if only because both were unexplainable and had touched his life within a few days of each other. It didn't *feel* like a coincidence.

He left the house, completely unsure of what to do next, and walked to his car. This time, he skirted the other side of the property, following the garage around to the driveway. As he came to the corner of the garage, where the white stucco met the blacktop in front and grass on the side, he found a couple of signs leaning against the wall. There were only a few things they could be: a political endorsement (which Viktoriya would never allow), credit to some kind of business that had serviced her property, or...

He picked one up and turned it over. And came face-to-face with four bold words.

FOR SALE BY OWNER.

He double-checked the address on the mailbox just to make sure he had broken into the right house as an insatiable need to find Joseph erupted in his chest and filled him with a suffocating panic he had no way of repelling.

13

AS TWILIGHT HANDED THE sky over to the night, Jack kept the car between the solid white lines—though barely conscious of the effort it took to do so. His mind was elsewhere, the nonsensical puzzle pieces of the last few days arguing on behalf of more eccentric theories that might, perhaps, better explain the recent changes in his life.

One of them was the "dream theory." Dream theory insisted he was still asleep, either still on the cruise ship with Stacey beside him, or perhaps even so far back as the night before they left for Miami, everything about the trip a dream. The problem with that theory, however, was that it disappeared into a sea of subjectivity so unsteady that there was no real way to tell how much of his past could be part of the dream. Maybe his whole marriage had been a concoction mixed by REM sleep. Maybe he was still in college, and this Stacey girl didn't even exist outside his imagination...a drug-induced coma after an accident he couldn't remember, or a head injury from a falling air-conditioning unit sustained during his walk to work. Maybe his entire life was a dream, and like so many science-fiction stories, he was actually hooked up to machines that were filling his mind with a false reality while they harvested his natural energy for the psychic aliens that now ruled earth.

Or maybe Mr. Sandman had grown bored of bestowing pleasant dreams on children and had ventured into a new market of darkness that now targeted adults. After all, Hans Christian Anderson's 1841 portrayal of the folk tale was a far cry from this torment. Yet something emerged from the recesses of his subconscious mind. A piece of text he'd long forgotten.

I will show you my brother. He is also called Ole-Luk-Oie but he never visits anyone but once, and when he does come, he takes him away on his horse, and tells him stories as they ride along. He knows only two stories.

One of these is so wonderfully beautiful, that no one in the world can imagine anything at all like it; but the other is just as ugly and frightful, so that it would be impossible to describe it...

There now, you can see my brother, the other Ole-Luk-Oie; he is also called Death.

That Jack could reel in any of the words from the depths of whatever brain lake they'd drowned in gave him pause. It didn't seem plausible that that should have happened, and it led to theory number two—the theory that Sandman's brother was suggesting. The one lobbing his mind back and forth like it was a birdie fluttering over the net of truth. The one that proclaimed he had never been rescued from the ocean. That no hand ever grabbed him at the last possible second.

That he was dead.

But (as he surely couldn't be in heaven) the concept of this being some kind of in-between, a testing ground for his soul or some sort of readiness exercise meant to prepare him for passage through the Pearly Gates, was also a theory with no practical use. If this was a supernal experience only, then the Joseph he was looking for didn't exist and neither did the wife he was mourning. Nothing was real at all. And if this wasn't real, if this wasn't a physical reality taking place on an objective plane of existence with true ramifications to be applied across actual time and space...then forget it. He'd just kill himself and save the misery of failing whatever test some pantheistic non-being called "Everything" had somehow and for some reason conjured up to amuse its unconscious self.

He needed a drink before his mind slipped down the hill of sanity and plunged headlong into this philosophic migraine. It was too much to try to grasp such things, reality itself a black hole full of infinite questions. Dark matter, quantum physics, string theory...

Jack shook his head. "Jesus Christ. Get a grip."

Jesus Christ. And suddenly, he knew why people like his wife chose to believe in nothing. It was easier to avoid the chaos, both philosophically and ethically. But such a belief system would lead him right back to the same irrational theories advising him that nothing was real, that it was all some scam, a random, meaningless mistake. There was no soul, no spirit, just the here and now and nothing forever. Love a chemical reaction in the brain; truth, beauty, and joy cruel fantasies produced by natural selection meant only to prolong the human species for...something. *Damn.* That was more depressing than the "why" and "how" questions.

He tried to stabilize the pillars of his sanity by smacking himself in the face. And in an instant, his world focused, the ivory towers of endless conjecture turning to sand and blowing away. He was back in his own driveway.

A drink. Now. Before I lose my marbles.

He knew that getting smashed wouldn't help find Joseph, but neither would winding up in a padded room, drooling all over himself for the rest of his life.

He shut the engine off, and the headlights fell away. After taking the key from the ignition, he pushed the door open and stepped out into the darkness.

He stood there and felt the cool night air glide through his hair. Smelled the freshly cut grass of nearby lawns. Listened to the strange cricket symphony. Watched fireflies blink yellow in the neighbor's yard. And in all of it, the reception of the perceived authenticity never wavered. Never gave way to a watery static as alien dream-gods tried better adjusting antenna REM. There were no giant arthropods crawling up the sides of the chimney, no deep-sea fish from hell swimming through the yard—though he did double-check to make certain they were fireflies blinking around him and not the glowing photophores of demon anglers.

Convinced for now that he wasn't asleep or dead, he continued to the house. But when he went to put the key into the keyhole, the door pushed open. Again. Only this time, he knew that he'd locked it.

He stepped back carefully. There was no car in the driveway, but he found a black, unmarked van with tinted windows parked in the street six doors away. His pulse quickened.

A noise came from inside.

Being the Jerry that he was, mentally prepared to survive anything from martial law to the super-virus that would wipe out mankind, he slipped his shoes off. He left them on the porch and eased the door open. Once inside, he closed it behind him without a noise.

The smell of kerosene hit him at once.

Kerosene? He thought of the kerosene heater he kept in the garage. But what would someone in a dark van parked halfway down the street want with his kerosene heater? If the person wanted to burn down his house, he'd be much better off using the gasoline in the garage rather than kerosene. But, though he knew that kerosene could never be hot enough to melt a hundred and ten stories of steel and concrete in fifty-six minutes, he sure knew that it could burn down his house. Just not as efficiently as gasoline.

As he tiptoed toward the stairs, he saw through the living room and noticed the interior door to the garage standing open in the kitchen. He raced up the stairs, silent in his socks, his heart thumping in his chest.

He entered the bedroom and ran to his closet, pulling a gun case from a shelf stacked with his independent newspapers. As he fumbled with the number lock, sweat began beading across his forehead. He finally got it open, grabbed the 9 mm Smith & Wesson out of the foam padding, and rammed home the seventeen-round magazine that he'd previously filled with hollow points. He moved the slide back and let go, the familiar sound of the first round being chambered startling him. This wasn't the shooting range.

Still hearing noises from the garage, but wary of more than one intruder, he descended the stairs, the pistol shaking ever so slightly in his grasp. He'd made it a point to visit the range every other month and had no qualms about his ability to use the gun on a target. But shooting a person would be something entirely different. Something he didn't really want to do—though he had a feeling that was what it was going to come down to.

As he approached the open garage door, he swept the sights back and forth throughout the house, waiting for someone else to appear. No one did. He stood with his back against the kitchen wall, the door open beside him, and took a few deep breaths. He suddenly wondered if he should call the police. It was a tempting thought, but one that wouldn't resolve the situation. By the time the police got here, he'd either be without a kerosene heater or in need of a different department.

He peered through the tiny space between the open door and its frame. Could see a person hunched over something on the floor, their back to him. He flexed his sweaty palms on the gun's plastic grip.

One. Two. Three...

He spun around past the door, brought the pistol up in one fluid motion, and aimed it down the few steps that led into the garage.

“Hey,” he cried out. “What are you doing?” But with the scene laid out before him now, he knew exactly what the guy was doing. And fear turned to fury.

The man turned around. He was dressed in jeans and a leather jacket and was reaching for something at his waist. Red containers of gasoline and blue bottles of kerosene sat scattered around his feet, the heater behind him. When he saw Jack standing there pointing the gun at him, his eyes flashed with recognition and then registered utter surprise. Then they went cold and he resumed drawing a gun.

Jack fired three times. The first shot buried itself in the man’s shoulder, the second his side, and the third seemed to miss entirely, chunks of concrete exploding off the far wall. But one of the two hits caused the guy to squeeze the trigger before he could get his gun clear, and he shot himself in the leg.

The man screamed but managed to raise his pistol and fire off three shots of his own as he fell.

Jack felt the first whiz past his head. He spun off to the side of the doorway and out of sight. He reached back around the doorframe and fired blindly into the garage. Another scream. He ran across the doorway, a shot ringing out after him as he cleared the opening and kicked the door shut. There was no other way out of the garage. The intruder either had to come through the door or bleed to death in the garage. But before Jack could position himself to cover the door, it flung open. It swung inches from his face and smashed against the wall, its gold handle punching a hole in the sheetrock.

As the man stumbled into the kitchen, rage eliminated Jack's ability to think and to strategize. He hurled himself at the stranger, tackling him down the short steps. The intruder took the brunt of the fall, landing on his back, his skull bouncing off the concrete floor. The gun flew out of his hand and skittered to a stop seven feet away.

Jack clambered to his knees and then sat all his weight on the man's chest. He began beating him in the face with the butt of his pistol. The gathering storms of confusion and pain had merged into a blind vehemence that was translating the person beneath him into the sole source of all his recent misery. So he continued pounding the hell out of him. Out of the masked men, the Nassau police, and ship security. Out of cancer and mammograms. Out of a consumer society that feasted on carcinogens and the greedy money makers that got off on it all. Out of an unforgiving, meaningless world that seemed bent only on destruction...

Jack screamed as a primal, animal frenzy pushed him to the brink of craze.

The man tried raising his hands to block the blows, but each strike left him more disoriented. Instead, he wrapped his hands around Jack's throat and squeezed with all the strength he had left.

Jack thought for sure the vise grip was about to crush his larynx. He tried to turn the gun around, to shoot the trespasser in the head. But he was already seeing stars and couldn't help dropping the gun and fighting the hands on his throat instead. But the strong, tattooed fingers around his neck wouldn't budge. So he stuck his thumb into the gunshot wound the guy had taken in the shoulder. A cry of pain echoed back, but the fingers didn't loosen. The man, despite his medium-looking frame, was strong as a bull and was giving every ounce of fortitude he could muster to squeezing Jack's head off.

Through his fading vision, Jack could just make out a blue one-liter bottle of kerosene lying in a stream of blood above the guy's head. He leaned into the death grip and reached out, got one finger on the bottle, and rolled it close enough to grab. The cap was off and kerosene was mixing with the blood, transforming the red stream into a pink, flammable lake. When he lifted the bottle, bringing it toward him, it leaked onto the face of the struggling man beneath him.

The intruder coughed and finally loosened his grip. And that was when Jack rammed the bottle right in there, jamming the nozzle halfway down his throat, kerosene dumping into his stomach and lungs.

The tattooed hands immediately went from Jack's throat to the bottle. The man gagged violently. Jack knew that ingesting half a liter of kerosene would be fatal, but he wasn't going to sit around and wait for the Reaper to sharpen his sickle on this one. He grabbed the pistol off the floor and managed to stand. He put the struggling criminal out of his misery by spreading the contents of his skull across the floor.

Jack couldn't move, could only stare at his work as his chest heaved and the toxic fumes dizzied his senses. And just like that, the storm passed. Like Legion cast out of the graveyard robber by Christ, he was himself again, the insanity falling off and dissipating through the floor—maybe seeking a herd of swine and a steep cliff, he wasn't sure. He stumbled backward up the stairs and fell into the kitchen. He hurried back to his feet, slammed the door shut. After staring at the blank door for a full minute, his mind racing, the adrenaline pumping, he willed himself to his feet and back into the garage, where he discovered that, yes, he had definitely shot the guy in the head.

He held his breath against the fumes and tried to ignore the gore splashed across the floor as he searched the guy's pockets for some kind of ID. None. He stood and looked around. It was obvious now what the guy's intent had been. Pouring gasoline from the red containers into the blue kerosene containers, he had planned on loading the heater with gas so that when he turned it on, the gasoline would explode, maybe even blow up the house. It would look like an idiot move by a homeowner who got his containers mixed up. Why anyone would use a heater this time of year, though, was a question he was sure nobody would've asked.

Jack counted the number of red and blue containers and was surprised to see that there were none extra. The guy had broken into his house and planned to burn it down with what was already in the garage. But how could he possibly have known about the kerosene heater and containers of gas? A probable calculation? But then, there was also the front door. Why come in the front door, where the whole neighborhood could see? Unless...

He left the garage, went through the kitchen, and began searching the living room.

There. On the mantel.

Jack walked over and picked up two keys joined by a metal loop. One said GM, the other... He pulled his own keys out of his pocket, found his house key, and held it up.

A perfect match.

Now he was certain that something was askew, some evil plot open and all its guts hanging out and stinking in his nostrils. It was a stench he was never supposed to get a whiff of, not from the bottom of the ocean. That was why the guy had been shocked to see him—he wasn't supposed to be there. He was supposed to be dead. He wondered if the kerosene man was one of the people who had thrown him overboard.

He noticed a black backpack resting against the wall below the living room window. He placed the 9mm on the mantel beside the keys and walked over to it. He picked it up, acknowledged its light weight, and unzipped it.

A paperback and a bundle of letters tied together with string.

He reached in, pulled out the book, and flipped it around so that he could see the title. *October's Ghost* by Ryne Douglas Pearson.

Ryne Douglas Pearson—*Simple Simon, Knowing*—the author Stacey had been reading on the boat.

A subtle alarm sounded in some remote section of intuition, but he ignored it and dropped the book back in the bag. He took out one of the letters and unfolded it.

Russian. It was all in Russian.

He pulled out another one. And another.

All Russian.

Agent Johnson would want to see this, but Jack wasn't convinced that the FBI would be any help. Maybe they would be; maybe they wouldn't. But what they sure wouldn't do was let him take matters into his own hands. They'd order him to sit home, to watch some television and wait. But he wasn't about to spend his days watching reruns of *Airwolf* while his family was out there somewhere. No way. So instead of calling Johnson or the police, he went back into the kitchen, opened the refrigerator, and took out a beer.

14

JACK HAD ALL THE windows open in the hopes that the kerosene's potent stench might be exorcized by the night air. So far, though, his drowsiness and headache had not dissipated.

Think. He took another gulp of beer, trying to recite what he knew for the hundredth time.

Masked men tossing him overboard *could* have been a case of mistaken identity, as he'd first assumed. But the person trying to burn down his house having a key, aware of what was in his garage, and recognizing him? That was no mistake. So the question became one of relation: were the two incidents connected? If so, then it could be appropriately determined that the men on the boat knew exactly who they were sending to the fishes. Had Viktoriya arranged the whole thing, trying to free her daughter of the great American idiot and spare Joseph from a life of fart jokes and baseball games? He didn't think so, but then again, her house was empty, and she was missing.

He leaned back in the easy chair, his eyes not on the living room around him but on the mental list he was again trying to assemble in his pounding head. He took a long sip and again tried to keep the pesky image of the dead guy still sprawled out in the garage from distracting him. He'd deal with that later.

He constructed a list in his head and ascended its shaky ladder one fact at a time. Nearing the top, he suddenly paused. He'd forgotten about this rung, and he tested it with a suspicious nudge. It was something that Johnson had gotten out of him, something he hadn't given much thought to before.

Stacey left the suite to send an email.

His fingers were clicking away over the keyboard, logging in to Stacey's email ten seconds later.

There was nothing in her sent folder younger than a week old.

He sat back and lifted the bottle again before bringing up the internet history. This time he was rewarded with road maps and directions to some place in upstate New York, email accounts he'd never heard of, and information on international flights.

Assuming the dead guy didn't order plane tickets from the house he was planning to blow up, Jack knew of no other person other than Stacey and Viktoriya who could've used the computer. But what would Stacey or Viki be doing checking out road maps to New York? And that thought added something else to his short list.

The FOR SALE signs. They had declared "Sale by Owner," yet, thinking back, Jack realized that the number advertised was not Viki's.

He'd have to drive back over in the morning and get the number.

Standing at the top of the ladder now, and with nothing but endless sky around him, he swiveled in the computer chair, picked up the Pearson book he'd taken from the backpack, and began thumbing through it. There, on the back page, was a block of Russian penmanship. Ryne Douglas Pearson...

He stood, tossed the book back onto the desk, and revisited the contents of Stacey's luggage that was still scattered across the bed. The other Pearson book was right beneath the top to one of her lingerie sets. *Simple Simon*. There were no notes in this one.

He collapsed onto the bed and into the pile of his wife's lingering scent, stared at the ceiling. Why would the intruder have a backpack filled with Russian letters and a novel—a Pearson novel no less?

The coincidence set the suicide note drifting across a territory of mysterious implication, and he decided that he would pay a visit to Stacey's doctor, too. He slipped into sleep, a myriad of images chasing after him—smashed faces, moonlit water, Joseph's twinkling eyes.

15

HE KICKS AS HARD as he can, but his legs are burning, and slowly, he begins to lose the ability to command them. Inky waters wash over his head, plunging him into the liquid abyss. He can sense the black eyes of finned predators watching him. His head breaks the surface again, but there's nothing in any direction. Only more waves. He is alone. His arms are prisoners shackled by fatigue and do as it demands—nothing. And this time, as he sinks beneath the choppy barrier that separates the two worlds, he knows he will never taste fresh air again. He sinks. And sinks. Lungs burning for the unreachable. "Stacey!" he screams.

It took a few moments for the world around him to focus, and only when it did could he finally catch his breath. Panting, he noticed the 9 mm resting on the bed beside him. So that hadn't been part of the dream. Then it all came rushing back. Stacey, Joseph, Viktoriya, the man in the garage, and what he'd planned to do today...whatever day today was.

He cocked his head to the side and looked out the window to see that rain was falling from an ash-gray sky. It made him sigh, and he stood up, walking unsteadily to the nearest window. He leaned against the frame and looked through the reflection of him scratching his stubbled jaw. It was still there, parked in the same spot—the black van.

He swore under his breath, understanding more clearly now that he had to call Johnson. This, whatever it was, was too much for him. Yes, the FBI would make him sit on his hands, but they were hands familiar with the keys of a calculator, so what chance did he really have at solving anything anyway? Running around looking for clues might make him feel better, but what was he supposed to do with the dead body in his garage? And the van it arrived in?

He undressed, picked out a clean pair of jeans and a red T-shirt from the pile on the bed, and dialed Agent Johnson. As the phone rang, he grabbed the pistol and stuck it into the belted waist of his pants. The clock hanging on the wall above his dresser read 10:30.

Voicemail.

"Agent Johnson, it's Jack Green. I, uh..." *blew a guy's brains out in my garage...* "Just call me as soon as you can. Thanks."

Then he took the long trip downstairs and back to the garage.

He opened the door, noting that the smell of kerosene was almost gone and was disappointed to find the dead guy still there. He had hoped the whole thing was a dream.

Thunder tumbled across the sky.

He shut the door on the corpse, never wanting to see it again, and walked to the kitchen window. He tried not to see Joseph's tiny body operating the vacant swing set, and instead let his mind wander back to the worn shovel lying beside the hole of missing clues. After a few deeper scoops, it found the letters.

The letters...

Jack pulled out his phone again, this time dialing Ivan.

"Ivan, it's Jack. You free at all today? I want to show you something. It's important. That's fine. Thanks. See you then."

Then Jack went and retrieved the stack of letters and the Pearson novel. He was almost to the front door when the mind-shovel, still working, struck something. Pausing, he brushed the dirt away from the subconscious discovery, anxious to know just what it was that was tugging at him.

The House of Thunder.

And he was running back to the bedroom.

Taking it from the pile on the bed, he flipped to its last page. A scribbled message in black ink stared up at him—one he remembered seeing but hadn't thought anything of at the time. It was the same Russian style from *October's Ghost*. But... He paused. *The House of Thunder* wasn't his novel—he'd found it lying around somewhere and had just tossed it in his bag for an escape on the cruise. It had to be Stacey's. But what would the intruder be doing with a Pearson book containing a Russian note penned by the same person who...

He went to the computer and brought up Amazon.com, fully aware that his internet activity was most likely being monitored by the FBI now. He'd only gotten a hundred pages into the Koontz novel, and it was so far a pretty decent thriller—though a supernatural or psychological one, he wasn't sure yet. He typed in the title and scrolled until finding a review that revealed nothing more than what he'd already discovered in the first hundred pages. At least not until its last couple of sentences.

> *...a Soviet plot seems to come out of nowhere and changes the story from a psychological thriller to a political thriller that some readers may associate with cold war paranoia...*

Soviet plot? Cold war paranoia? He'd suspected a ghost story.

He scrolled back to the search bar and this time typed *October's Ghost* into the search bar. The screen switched to the details of the Pearson novel. The product description suggested a premise built on Castro still having possession of an October nuke that leads to the US and Russia bracing for another nuclear standoff.

According to the novels' product details, the books had been published in 1988 and 1994. Though that didn't necessarily mean anything. At least nothing that could explain the kerosene man having a book from the same series as Stacey's current read and it containing a similar Russian message as that of her *House of Thunder*. Coincidence? The Jerry in him didn't believe in coincidences.

Then realization struck home and stiffened his back. He should've checked the whole house last night to see if anything else was out of place, to see what else the man had come to do. Because he knew now that he hadn't just come to burn it down.

He began walking through his home, the bag and its contents ultimately bringing him into Stacey's closet and confirming his unconfessed suspicion that the books and letters had not been brought *into* the house. His eyes danced over her hanging clothes, and suddenly she was there with him, wearing every one of them. He ignored the stinging in his eyes and moved his gaze back and forth, looking for anything out of place.

The fluorescent bulb above him flickered. He raised his eyes...and saw that the air vent in the ceiling was unscrewed and slightly ajar.

He stepped up onto a wall shelf full of shoes, reached up and pressed against the rectangular grid, popping it up and into the ceiling. He pushed it aside, moving it so that it was lying to the left of the hole and resting on top of the ceiling. There was nothing attached to it, no ductwork slithering through the open space and distributing either heat or cold throughout the house. He slipped his hand into the hole and felt around. Just an empty space above the ceiling. Strange. He reached in further, standing on his toes and straining.

His middle finger brushed something.

Gaining a few more centimeters, he was able to pull whatever it was toward the opening. When he could finally grab it, he hopped down off the shelf with it in his hand.

Another book. *Seventeen Moments of Spring* by Yulian Semyonov.

He never heard of it, but something fluttered to the carpeted floor at his feet when he opened its cover. Bending over, he picked up a black-and-white photograph of a man. There was Russian written across the back of it. He opened to the back of the book and found more Russian handwriting staring up at him.

He slammed the book shut and swore. It didn't take a genius to figure out where the backpack's contents had come from.

He left the bedroom, put everything back in the pack, and slung it over his shoulder. Before leaving, however, he first stopped in front of a modest bookshelf much smaller than the one containing his books on government conspiracy, the global elite, politics, and secret societies. These were all novels, and mostly Stacey's. He pulled one out after another, thumbing through the pages before tossing them over his shoulder and into a pile on the floor. None had messages in them.

When he stepped outside, finally ready to revisit the address that had belonged to his mother-in-law just a week ago, he heard an engine screaming and turned his head just in time to see a black sedan come speeding down the street. He saw the rear window slide down a few inches and a cylindrical object poke through the widening gap.

It was a scene he'd seen in many movies, and given the downward turn his life had suddenly taken, there was no hesitating. He dove to the ground as the silent bullets smacked into the door above him. Then, rolling behind a bush that stood to the side of the walkway, he withdrew the 9 mm from his pants.

It was too late. The sedan was gone.

But then came a new sound echoing down the street and through the rain. The dead guy's van was pulling away from the curb and coming toward him. He jumped to his feet and jogged across the front yard. He raised the pistol and fired four times in reckless fury as the vehicle passed. It disappeared around the bend at the end of the street, four holes now lining its side.

Jack sprinted to the car, tossed the gun on the passenger seat, and threw the Hyundai in reverse with smoking tires. After whipping it into the street, he jammed the car into drive. He noticed his neighbor, Steve, standing wide-eyed and slack-jawed, staring at him from his mailbox, newspaper in hand.

Jack slammed on the gas and shot to the main road, but the van was nowhere to be seen.

He swore and slammed the steering wheel over and over again.

"*What is happening?*" he screamed again.

16

JACK PULLED INTO Viktoriya's driveway, and his eyes darted suspiciously about the property that had been so familiar to him. When his phone sounded in his pants, he nearly jumped through the windshield.

"Hello?" he answered after wrestling the phone from his pocket.

It was Agent Johnson.

Jack took a deep breath. "I think you need to get over to my place. The front door's unlocked. Just...check the garage." He paused before adding, "It was self-defense."

A string of questions began dripping from the phone's tiny speaker, but Jack didn't have time for an interrogation right now. "Look, I have to meet someone, but I'll call you as soon as I'm done. I think I do need your help." He hung up.

He took the gun off the passenger seat and stepped into the rain. The signs were still there leaning against the house. He hadn't dreamed that either—unless, of course, his waking up was part of the dream. He shrugged off the Sandman nonsense once more, finding it strange that the old folk tale's suggestion was so persistent, and punched the sign's phone number into his phone.

Suddenly wary of how he might appear to a passerby—standing there at the side of an empty house in the rain, phone in one hand, gun in the other—he trotted back to the car. His clothes were soaked and clinging to him, and chills were rattling his body. He set the pistol back on the seat beside him and turned on the heat. Then he hit the send button on the cell.

"*Hello?*" a man's voice answered.

"Hi, I'm looking for Viktoriya Arsov."

A pause. "*And how did you come by this number?*"

Jack didn't see what would be lost by stating the truth, so he just said it. "Actually, this is her son-in-law. Her house is empty, and she isn't answering her cell. I got this number from the sale signs. Can you tell me what's going on?"

"*You're her son-in-law, you say?*"

"That's right."

"*Well, Mr. Son-In-Law, how is it that you didn't know she was moving, huh? Your wife is her daughter, no? You expect me to believe that she doesn't know when her mother is moving? And if she does know this, then I have to wonder why she hasn't told you, no? How do I know you aren't some crazy stalker person looking to cut Viki's throat? How do I know she didn't move to get away from you? You could be a serial killer, no?*"

"What? No. What the—"

The accented man continued, "*Well, I own the house. Your so-called 'mother-in-law' was only renting it from me.*"

The statement slapped him with surprise, its handprint lingering. "How long?" he stammered.

"*How long?*"

"Did she rent from you?"

"*Goodbye, Mr. Son-In-Law. I suggest you speak with—*"

"She's dead," he blurted.

The man on the other line didn't hang up, but silence occupied the line for a few seconds. "*And when did this happen?*" he finally asked.

"A few days ago. We were on a cruise. She went overboard. Viktoriya was watching my son, Joseph, at our house. When I got home, they weren't there. So I came here. Wherever she went, she took my son."

"*Even if I did believe you were not a serial killer, I couldn't help you anyway. I do not know where she went. I was going to sell the place, but now someone else is stepping up to rent.*"

"Did she give you notice?"

"*Yes. About one month.*"

"Thanks." Then, in an attempt to validate his claim, he added, "The FBI may be in touch." He tossed the phone on the seat next to the gun. He stared past the windshield. Everything was incomprehensible, the rain, like the gathering clues, splashing off the glass and distorting his view.

The cell rang again, cutting through the storm's rhythmic beat tapping against the roof of the car.

"Yeah?"

It was Ivan. He was waiting for him.

"I'll be right there."

WITH THE 9 MM left behind in the glove compartment, Jack splashed through the puddles that spotted the parking lot, not caring to spend the extra time avoiding them. When he opened the heavy glass door, the smell of Starbucks coffee greeted him, as did a warm and cozy environment. He spotted Ivan at a table in the back corner. There was no line of coffee vampires shouting out their blood orders in paragraphs, so he was able to order without delay. A bold venti seemed to be what he needed, and as he handed over a five-dollar bill, he couldn't keep his hand from shaking.

"Thanks," he said to the person handing him his drink. He took it to Ivan.

"So what's all this about?" Ivan asked before Jack could even sit down.

As he sat, letting the backpack slip off his shoulder, Jack looked around the small shop. Only three other people were present, all positioned at tables and engrossed in their own private worlds. One was on a laptop, one was reading a paperback—which, Jack was relieved to see, was the newest King novel and not another episode from that Ryne Douglas Pearson series—and the last was hiding behind an open newspaper. “Have they been here long?” he whispered.

Ivan looked confused. “Before I got here.” He laughed nervously. “Jack, if this is about that GMO rice with the human DNA I told you about...”

“It’s not.” He brought the backpack up and retrieved its contents, placing them on the table between them.

“What’s this?” Ivan asked.

“It’s all in Russian. Can you read them?”

He picked up *October’s Ghost* and began flipping through it. “This is English, buddy.”

Jack didn’t smile. Instead, he snatched the book and promptly opened it to the scribbled message in back.

Ivan read it. “‘What a wild idea this one is, my precious Anna! I truly do love these stories. We should take pen to paper ourselves one day!’” Ivan looked up. “Who’s Anna?”

But Jack just pushed the Koontz book toward him. “Same spot.”

After a furtive glance at his friend, Ivan read the note in *The House of Thunder*. “‘This one truly was thrilling. Oh, that it might be so! I should send the...’” His eyes bolted up.

"What?" Jack asked, leaning against the table.

"'I should send the *Kremlin* this one, my love!'" he finished. "Jack, what is this?"

"There's one more book." He handed over *Seventeen Moments of Spring.*

"A classic," Ivan stated, taking the work in his hands.

Jack took a gulp of his coffee. "What is it?" His hands were still shaking.

"It's a story set in 1945 about a Soviet spy operating in Nazi Germany. It's considered by a lot of people to be the greatest Soviet spy novel ever written."

"Open it."

Ivan did as instructed, and had no trouble locating the glossy black-and-white picture. "You know him?"

"No."

"Where did you get it?"

"Found it in my house." Jack impatiently signaled for his friend to get on with the interpreting.

"Okay," he said, unsure. He squinted back down at the note. "'My dear Anna, I love you more than anything else. I hope you know that. Remember me always and know that you will always be in my heart. I wish our lot in life had been a better one, but at least I was able to share a time with you.'"

Jack took another sip and turned his eyes to the parking lot. The rain was lashing the windows, drowning the light music coming from the speakers above them.

"The note in the back of this one," Ivan said, pointing to the novel, "just says 'hope you like this as much as I did.'"

"And these." Jack rested the stack of letters on the table.

"Oh, come on, Jack. You want me to read *all* these to you?"

"Just tell me what they are."

Ivan sipped his own coffee concoction before working pages from a random envelope. A few minutes passed in silence before he selected two more to read from.

All of a sudden, Ivan looked uncomfortable, squirming awkwardly in his chair.

"What?" Jack demanded.

"They're letters from a guy named Vadim to this Anna girl."

"What do they say? Why would Stacey keep them hidden in her closet?"

"She had them hidden in her closet?"

"Yeah."

"I have no idea. Maybe she's holding them for a friend of hers."

"I don't know any Anna. Are there any dates?"

"2005 through 2006," he told him.

"The year before I met Stacey."

He looked down at the letter still in his hands and was about to say something, but apparently changed his mind. "Jack," he said instead, "why don't you just tell me what is going on?"

So he did. Everything from the cruise to Viktoriya's landlord.

Ivan looked incredulous. "You were just shot at outside your own house?" He was scanning the parking lot now, too.

"It's funny, you know what my first thought was with these books?" Jack asked.

"What?"

He began laughing. "That it was some *Catcher in the Rye* thing."

"You mean from *Conspiracy Theory*? The CIA programming Jerry to always need a copy?"

Jack nodded. "Look what you've done to me. You got me thinking my wife is a Russian spy programmed to buy Soviet-themed novels."

But Ivan wasn't laughing. After a deep breath and a moment to reevaluate the content of the letters in light of his friend's story, he said, "The letters allude to something that the Vadim guy is involved in. Something he promises to find a way out of so that they can be together again."

Jack's smile faded. "Vadim and Anna."

"They seem to be married. Now he never comes right out and says what it is he's involved with, but it's clear that it's the reason they're not together."

"Something like..."

"Like SVR crap."

"SVR? As in Russian foreign intelligence?"

Ivan ran a hand through his black hair, nodding. "As in the FSB's Foreign Intelligence Service, yes."

"The FSB being—"

"The new KGB."

Jack looked confused. "I thought..."

"The KGB was disbanded in 1991 with the collapse of the Soviet Union. In 1995, it was restructured into the Ministry of Security, the Federal Service of Counterintelligence, and the Federal Security Service—or FSB. But in 1998, Yeltsin appointed Putin, who of course was KGB, to head up the FSB. When Putin became president in 2000, he began siphoning power back into the intelligence services, the FSB drawing all kinds of other departments beneath the umbrella of its own directive, many of them just old KGB departments renamed.

They said the KGB was a state within a state, but the FSB, in many ways, has *become* the state. Ruthless and more powerful than the KGB ever was. Or maybe that's just Western paranoia. I don't know."

Jack slowly removed the lid from his cup and began to swirl its contents. He stared into the blackness as if the key to understanding everything was at the bottom of the paper cup and he needed only to catch a glimpse of it to set everything in place. When no revelation came, he looked up to his Russian friend. "Is it possible that you could be overreacting?"

Ivan's slightly rounded face brightened into a smile, but the conviction in his brown eyes did not change. "It's possible that your story tainted my objectivity. But masked men, missing family, guns and intrigue..." He shrugged. "It's hard not to make the leap. A guy tried to burn down your house, Jack, and he had these books with him. I think it's safe to say you're in the middle of something."

"You think the guy in the photo is Vadim?"

"I don't know. I guess."

They sat in silence for a few minutes, Ivan letting Jack wrestle with the information.

"So," Jack finally began, "the man in my house was taking those..." He indicated the pile of letters and books on the table.

"Or he was planting them."

"No. There wasn't any evidence to suggest that the hole in the ceiling was recent. No drywall dust—"

"Did you check your vacuum?"

Jack snorted under his breath and leaned back in his chair, lifting the cup to his lips again while setting his gaze on the rain.

Ivan leaned forward. "You have no idea what's going on. What these letters are. Where they came from. Who they're to. What the books mean. Why you were thrown overboard. What happened to Stacey. Why Viktoriya would take Joseph somewhere..." He trailed off, sitting back himself. "And if I can be totally honest, you didn't really know who Stacey was before you married her."

Jack squinted. "What does that mean?"

"It means that those letters, regardless of who they're from and for, suggest something...big."

"You think Stacey is—"

"Not who you think she is," he stated bluntly. "Or maybe was."

Jack was so shocked by the statement that he couldn't respond.

"You don't know what she used to be involved in, who her old friends were. We've talked about this before, Jack. When it comes to Stacey's past, you know next to nothing."

"What are you saying?"

"That for now you concentrate on finding Joseph. If these letters belong to Stacey, then she has them for a reason. Maybe she's involved somehow, at least in that she's aware of what's going on. Maybe whatever Vadim was involved in has run its course, and now he's cleaning up."

"You mean..."

"I don't know what I mean. Just...find your son."

But before Jack could think of another response, his phone rang. He fished it out of his pocket and accepted the call, irritated at the untimely interruption. He knew that Ivan wasn't telling him everything, that he had a theory he wasn't sharing. "Hello?" His eyes swung down, dropping away from his friend. His face turned ashen, and his mouth opened with a silent gasp. "What?" He listened to the voice on the other end for another second. "I'll be right there."

Concern flooded Ivan's face. "What is it?"

"My house is on fire."

17

FOR TWO MILES, JACK could only stare at the pillar of smoke rising above the earth—a dark beacon signaling a disaster that he was powerless to quell. He beeped his horn, swerved around slow traffic, and pushed the Hyundai harder than it had ever been pushed before. But in the end, parked alongside the curb a few houses down, rescue vehicles littering the street with flashing lights shining through the rain and groups of people standing around under umbrellas, he could only watch his house—*their* house—fall apart beneath an ominous, bright-orange flame. The firemen were sending streams of arching water into the dancing blaze, but even with the falling rain, it was a lost cause.

He watched, unable to truly believe what he was seeing. Joseph's room. His and Stacey's things. The photo albums. Their life.

A knock on the glass startled him.

"Jack?"

His cop friend was peering down through the window. At first Jack thought he was some murky apparition sent to usher him into the next world, his form ghostly and veiled beneath the downpour. Jack finally acknowledged him by lowering the window. "Hey, Don."

Donny leaned closer, the falling water splashing off his rain jacket and spraying the car's interior. "Jack, your neighbor's telling people that you were shooting at someone..." There was worry in his voice, though his eyes were too busy blinking away waterfalls to get a read on them. "What's going on?" He was whispering, his eyes darting through the gathered audience as if at any moment someone might discover his friend's presence and lead a charge toward the car.

"Wanna take a ride?"

"You know I can't. Tell me what's going on. First Stacey's missing, and then you're shooting at people and your house is on fire..."

Jack stared straight ahead, not really wanting to rehash the entire string of disjointed events again. So instead, he asked, "Is Agent Johnson here?"

Donny frowned. "Yeah, he's over there." He pointed into the flashing chaos. "Listen, Jack, I don't know what you're—"

"Do me a favor, Don?" Jack cut him off. He reached into the backpack and took out the picture he'd found in *Seventeen Moments of Spring*. "See if you can find out who this guy is. I think his name is Vadim. He's Russian."

Donny stared at him a second. "You're not going to tell me?"

"Later. I promise."

His high school friend took the picture and slid it into the dry safety of a zippered pocket. "Why don't you give it to Johnson?"

After a moment of consideration, Jack shrugged. "Do you trust him?"

Snickering, Donny asked, "You mean do I think he's into illegal wiretaps, hunting down income tax protestors, and labeling anyone capable of independent thought a terrorist?"

Jack shot him an impatient look.

"Yeah, I trust him."

"Okay. But still." He motioned toward the pocket the picture had disappeared into. "Can you find out for me?"

He sighed. "I'll see what I can do, Jack. You'd better tell me what the hell is going on though. And soon."

"I'll call you once this is all cleared up."

"All right. But go talk to Johnson now before local snatches you up." Then, before turning to leave, he asked, "Hey, you're not in trouble, are you? I mean—"

"With the law?" He shook his head, watching as a section of his house collapsed into a shower of sparks. "Not yet."

"Not yet?"

"Don, I'll call you later." He put the window up, blocking the splashing rain from further soaking his car. Then he opened the door and got out. "I don't know what's going on, Don. But I think it's big. And somehow Stacey was—*is*—in the middle of it." He turned and went after the FBI man. "I'll call you later. Find out who that guy is," he called back over his shoulder.

Jack found Johnson standing alone, leaning against a fire truck and observing the inferno that was converting all of his possessions to ash. It seemed like the agent was searching the pluming clouds for clues.

"Agent Johnson," Jack said.

Without turning toward him, Johnson quietly asked, "Would you like to explain why your house is on fire? And what you thought I should see in your garage?"

"I shot an intruder last night," he said.

Johnson's gaze swept away from the bonfire and settled on Jack's face. "Excuse me?"

Trusting Donny's friendship with the federal agent, Jack told him everything. The incident in the garage, the backpack, Viktoriya's house, the drive-by...

Johnson shook his head. "You should've reported it. It doesn't look good, you killing a guy in your house and not calling it in. No matter how you spin it."

"I know. I wasn't thinking clearly."

"We could've found out who the guy was." He nodded toward the house. "Now we have nothing." He put his hands on his hips and exhaled. "Let me have the letters and books."

Jack handed over the backpack.

After taking it, Johnson said, "I talked to the cruise line this morning. They're checking on the tapes. I also checked all your internet accounts. Someone was online getting driving directions north."

"Yeah, I saw that."

They both stood silent for a moment. "Jack," Johnson started, "I don't know who's going to be getting involved with this or what they'll uncover. There are witnesses who saw you shooting at a passing vehicle, your house is on fire, your wife is missing, your son and mother-in-law are missing..." He turned and looked him in the eye. "People are going to have some questions for you. If they find a corpse in there with bullet holes in it, those questions are going to be coming sooner rather than later. I won't be able to help you the way that I am once that happens. Official channels will have to be opened and protocol followed. Everything will slow down, and you'll be the number one suspect."

"If they're burning the house to cover something up, then they wouldn't take the van and leave the body."

Johnson nodded. "Do you even have a license to carry that pistol?"

"Of course."

"If you want to find your family, then you have to be smart about this. Either that or you can spend your time phoning lawyers. Do you have anywhere you can stay? Family?"

"No family."

"Talk to Donny, then. You'll be safer with him anyway, and he can keep you out of trouble." He started walking away, the backpack hanging from his grasp. "I'll call you as soon as I have something."

"Hey," Jack called after him.

Johnson turned.

"Why are you doing this? Helping me, I mean?"

"Let's just say I owe Donny a couple of favors." And then he pointed a finger at him. "But that only goes so far, Mr. Green. If you want my help, you have to observe the boundaries. If you start going all Liam Neeson, then I'll have to step away and let the bureau take over."

Jack nodded his understanding and watched him walk away, rainwater dripping off his face. He turned his attention back to the house he and Stacey had bought four years ago, right before Joseph was born. Thirsty flames were dancing through the broken windows, licking cool droplets out of the sky as smoke continued to rise like a pagan offering, his family the sacrifice required for atonement. But why?

Anger began to boil in Jack's veins. Someone had thrown him overboard. Someone had taken his wife. Someone had shot at him. Someone just burnt down his house...

One way or another, regardless of Johnson's warning, someone was surely going to pay.

The orange-red fire that was reflecting off his hypnotized eyes reached down and ignited something inside him that he'd only recently met.

Rage.

18

JACK OPENED THE DOOR to the doctor's office and stepped in, quickly observing the waiting room as he strode to the reception counter. Only one elderly woman was present in the small room, her face stuck in a magazine. A talk show sounded softly from a TV on the wall.

"Can I help you?" came a voice from behind the counter.

As Jack got closer to the source of the voice, he saw a young blonde woman looking up from a computer.

"Yeah. I'd actually like to speak to Dr. Timonen, my wife's primary."

"What's your wife's name, sir?"

"Stacey Green."

"And you are?"

"Jack."

"Are you a patient here as well, Mr. Green?" Her fingers were clicking away over the keyboard.

"I've been here a few times."

She looked up at him again. "May I ask what this is about?"

"I just have some questions about her cancer."

His statement seemed to startle her, and all the normal questions he'd seen in her eyes scattered instantly. "Uh..." She squinted and looked back over her shoulder to a female doctor who had just stepped into the office. "Dr. Kelly, this is Mr. Green. Stacey's husband," the receptionist said.

Dr. Kelly lifted her eyes and smiled. "Jack."

He nodded and managed a polite smile of his own.

The doctor stepped up to the counter and extended her hand. "Michelle Kelly. I've heard a lot about you. Your wife is a wonderful woman. You're lucky to have her." She shook his hand.

A lump formed in Jack's throat. "Yeah..."

She sensed his unease and tilted her head, her eyebrows pinching. "Is everything okay?"

The receptionist said, “He’s here to talk to Dr. Timonen. About Stacey’s *cancer*.”

Dr. Kelly looked like she’d been slapped in the face. “Cancer?”

“Yeah...”

“Uh.” She looked around before lowering her voice. “Dr. Timonen isn’t in today. Hasn’t been in for a couple of days, actually. No one can seem to get a hold of him.”

“He’s missing?”

She studied him for a second. “Why don’t you come on back, Mr. Green.” She motioned for him to walk through the door beside the counter.

He followed her into a room and sat down in a chair beside the single desk. Pictures of the human body and some of its specific ailments decorated the walls. The bed with the paper lining was in the room’s opposite corner.

Dr. Kelly crossed her legs. “How is Stacey?”

“Uh...” He sighed as he searched for an answer that wouldn’t require a repeat of the entire story. “I’m not exactly sure.”

Alarm crossed the soft features of her face. “Did something happen?”

“We were on a cruise.”

She uncrossed her legs and stiffened as if she had a sense of what was coming.

"I was thrown overboard."

"What?"

"Obviously, they saved me. But Stacey's missing."

"Oh my God." Her hand flew to her mouth, and the pleasant softness of her face fell away like a melting mask.

"We just wanted to have a good time, you know, before the cancer took over our lives."

She wagged her head, her red ponytail swaying back and forth as tears formed in her eyes. After taking a few moments to compose herself, she said, "I don't understand. Who told you she had cancer?"

"She did. Timonen did. Check her file. Her mammogram came back positive."

"She had the hospital send the results here?"

He shrugged.

"Hold on a sec, will you?" She sniffled and rubbed her swollen eyes as she stood and left the room.

Jack sat waiting for almost ten minutes. He spent the time pondering his conversation with Johnson and questioning his own theory that his house was burnt down to cover something up. What would someone want to cover up? The picture and the novels? Who would they threaten? How? And then there were the letters and whatever Ivan wasn't telling him. Something to do with the SVR and FSB. Something that made even less sense.

When Dr. Kelly came back in the room, she had a bunch of files and big envelopes tucked under her arm. She didn't apologize for making him wait. Instead, she wordlessly extracted one of two white envelopes and handed it to him. She set the remainder of the pile down on the desk and crossed her arms.

Jack pulled the glossy films from the packet and held them up to the light. "These hers?"

"Her name is on it. They were in her file." She wiped a teardrop from one of her eyes. "At least that's what it says."

Jack looked confused. "What do you mean?"

She handed him the other envelope. "Has she had a biopsy yet?"

He shook his head. "No."

"Then you don't know for certain that the mass is malignant."

He shook his head again, the look on his face growing more and more uncertain. "I don't understand."

"What exactly did Stacey tell you?"

He thought back, the new envelope still sitting unopened on his lap. "Uh... She got a phone call from Dr. Timonen one day. I guess instead of the letter she usually gets when the results are normal."

She nodded for him to continue.

"He told her the mammogram showed a mass and that she should have a biopsy right away. She thought it was strange because he hadn't detected anything during the physical exam. Apparently, from what he told her, the mass was pretty significant."

She pointed to the images he'd already removed, at a large white circle that looked like some lunar lake in an old satellite photo. "It's very big," she confirmed.

He stared at it for a while. It was, after all, the very reason they were on the ship in the first place. "She went to pick up the images, to drop them off at the biopsy place and schedule her appointment. I think she had to sign for them. They told her not to open the envelope, that it was for the doctor's eyes only. Of course she opened it as soon as she got in the car. Who wouldn't? There was a piece of paper along with the images. It said, 'Biopsy ordered to confirm malignancy.'"

"But she never actually had the biopsy?"

"No. She never even dropped the images off. They're still in her closet..." He trailed off, remembering that there was no such place anymore.

"I don't understand," Dr. Kelly said. "Why was she so certain she had cancer?"

"Because Timonen told her she did. The radiologist was ninety-five percent sure. Thus the note."

"I didn't know anything about this," she stated suspiciously.

"Were you supposed to?" Jack asked.

"No. But I'm pretty close to your wife. Dr. Timonen is her primary, but she's seen me just as much as she's seen him over the years. And I would think Dr. Timonen would've told me if he was sure she had cancer."

"Well, I guess he didn't."

She nodded toward the contents in his hands. "Open the other one."

Without question, he dumped more black-and-white film into his lap. "I'm not sure what I'm looking at here."

"Your wife's breasts, Jack."

His eyes met hers. "I know. What about them?"

"How big are they?"

Her use of the present tense seemed forced, but Jack was able to circumnavigate the insinuation. “Her breasts?”

“Yeah.”

He shrugged. Under any other circumstances, he might have blushed, and he remembered the verses from Song of Solomon that he’d quoted over dinner the last night he’d been with her. “Big enough.”

Pointing at the images, Dr. Kelly asked, “You see any evidence of a mass in those?”

He sighed, holding it up. There was definitely no moon lake on this planet’s topography. “When were these from?”

“The previous mammogram.”

“That’s kind of fast, isn’t it? For a mass to form that big?”

“What concerns me more than that, Jack, is that those breasts”—she pointed to the normal film—“are not these breasts.” She moved her finger to indicate the other images.

Jack held up one of each, comparing them.

“I don’t have to be a radiologist to tell the difference between a B-cup and a double D.”

He looked at the images again. "What the hell are you telling me?"

"Have you noticed Stacey's breasts shrinking?"

"No."

"Then the film with the mass can't be Stacey's. Besides, a mass that big would be detectable during a routine exam. Timonen would know this." She shook her head. "I don't know how the images could've gotten mixed up. Or how Timonen missed it." She grew silent. "It doesn't make sense."

But Jack was a step ahead of her. "And you said no one knows where Timonen is?"

She nodded, her eyes distant. Then they focused, and she looked at him. "Your wife doesn't have breast cancer, Jack."

STACEY DOESN'T HAVE CANCER... He should be jumping for joy through the parking lot, dancing in the rain and singing at the top of his lungs. If, of course, the implications weren't so dark. As much as he wanted to believe that the whole thing was just an innocent mix-up —Stacey's images getting switched with someone else's—it simply wasn't a piece of the puzzle that fit anywhere. As Dr. Kelly had said, Timonen would never have missed it. And now he was MIA, too. What happened on the ship had been planned in advance, the masked men boarding in Miami with a specific mission to carry out. And the cancer was the very setup for the cruise.

But the whole *idea* of taking a cruise was...Viktoriya's. She, in fact, had even paid for it. And she had packed up and disappeared with Joseph.

He dialed Donny as he pulled out of the parking lot, his heart thumping in his chest.

Voicemail.

"Hey, Don, it's Jack. Listen, I need to talk to you. Call me back as soon as you can." He ended the call just as another was coming in. "Hello?"

"*Pull over.*"

"What?"

"*It's Johnson. I'm right behind you. Pull over at the McDonald's.*"

Jack looked into the rearview mirror and saw a black Ford sedan flashing its lights at him. He slowed and pulled into the driveway, coming to a stop beneath the famous golden arches.

Johnson came running up alongside the passenger door and was knocking on the window before Jack could get the pistol out of the glove compartment. He motioned for Jack to unlock the door. He slid into the seat and out of the rain. After taking a second to adjust his jacket and tie, he turned and faced Jack. "I heard back from the cruise line."

"Yeah?"

"The tapes were erased."

"What?"

Johnson stopped him by holding up a hand. "I know. I also had someone check on your wife's cell. There's no signal at all, which it creates even when it's off. I pulled the phone records and got the person who texted your wife's phone the night of..." He trailed off, not wanting to walk Jack back through those moments.

Jack nodded, saving him from having to finish the thought.

"It wasn't Vadim, but it was registered to a Russian male. Coincidence?"

Jack took a deep breath. A Russian man sends some bizarre text to his wife hours before they're abducted? He couldn't help but think of the FSB and wondered again what Ivan was keeping from him. "Did someone review the letters yet?"

"Someone's working on it as we speak."

He debated whether or not to tell him about Ivan and his SVR theory, and ultimately decided to sit on it for now, to see what the FBI came up with on its own.

"One of your mother-in-law's credit cards was used at a gas station in Connecticut," Johnson said.

Viktoriya... "The cruise was her idea," Jack said. And when Johnson didn't respond, Jack turned. "My wife didn't have cancer. Her mammogram results were switched or doctored. And now her primary is missing."

"You just find that out?" he asked, nodding toward the doctor's office half a mile behind them.

"Yeah."

Johnson fell silent, his gaze again locked in the distance as if there were answers hidden in the gray sky. "Donny trusts me, Jack. You should, too."

Jack was taken aback by the comment. "I *am* trusting you."

"Donny came to a dead end with the picture you gave him. So he sent it to me. I know you don't trust me like you trust him, but—"

"Trust you the same way I trust one of my best friends? You're one of *them*, Agent Johnson. Ruby Ridge, Wacco, Oklahoma City, the World Trade Center —"

Johnson sighed. "I'm not one of *them*, Jack. But..."

"But what?"

"You have a decision to make, so let's look at what we know so far. Your wife doesn't have cancer. The person who told her she did is missing. Your mother-in-law sets you up on a cruise. Three masked men throw you off the ship, and your wife disappears after writing a suicide note. The ship's security tapes are erased. Your mother-in-law takes off with your son. Someone with a key to your house tries to burn it down after removing certain things of Stacey's. Someone shoots at you. Someone *does* burn down your house..."

Jack nodded, but it sounded like the stupidest thing he'd ever heard. This wasn't some badly scripted TV movie, this was his life. It was happening to him. "What's your point?"

"I passed the picture along. It's not the Vadim in the letters. This man was a KGB agent who died in 1982."

If the entire solar system crash-landed in his lap, Jack wouldn't have been more surprised. "Are you telling me that my wife kept a picture of a dead KGB agent hidden in her closet?"

Johnson sighed. "I don't know what else I'll be able to uncover on my own,

Jack. That picture is raising eyebrows in the bureau, and it won't be long before other agencies get a whiff of what I'm digging up. So here's where you have to make a choice. Either drop this thing now and let all the dots remain unconnected and focus on finding your son…or let me open up an official FBI investigation."

He thought about it. "What else could you do?"

"Not much. And anything I do is going to take time. I'm relying on favors here. It could take me weeks to find Viktoriya's car. Or it could take me hours with official support."

"And once it's official…"

"You have to back down and wait things out, and…" He ran a hand through his hair. "You're going to have to endure those tough questions we talked about before."

He threw the door open and swung his feet around, planting them in a puddle. "Think about it. You've got an hour to make up your mind."

"What do you think I should do?"

The FBI agent looked right into his eyes. "Honestly, if I were in your shoes, I would be mostly concerned with finding my son. And then, depending on what I believed was going on, I'd either want my wife back or I wouldn't." He stepped into the wetness, and thunder rolled across the heavens.

Jack didn't notice the door slam shut or Johnson's sedan roar past him. He was in another world, one connected by a satirical, golden-arched gateway.

"I'd either want my wife back or I wouldn't..."

What was that supposed to mean?

19

FOR THE NEXT TWO hours, Jack sat alone in a diner and waited for Donny to call him back. He had no appetite to speak of but somehow managed to force a bacon omelet into his stomach. The coffee, however, had no trouble going down and kept coming. He was on his sixth cup, and his mind was spinning in circles while his foot tapped impatiently on the tile floor beneath the table. He wanted to be doing something. But he was stuck with "waiting" and thought he might explode, spontaneously combust into a cloud of frustration.

For a moment, he had considered just driving to Connecticut. But that was a stupid idea. Was he going to walk the state asking random pedestrians if they'd seen an old Russian lady with a four-year-old boy? It might feel better than sitting here doing nothing, but it wouldn't accomplish an iota more. So instead, he thought of the choice Johnson gave him, about the cryptic message he'd exited with. And it was halfway through coffee cup number two—an hour after Johnson had left him in the McDonald's parking lot—that the agent called asking for his decision. And Jack had given it to him.

He needed to find Stacey and Joseph as fast as possible, and obviously, his background in sales didn't qualify him for that sort of mission. So he relented and gave Johnson permission to make his investigation official. But that didn't mean he intended to sit around idle like this while the FBI got in a pissing match with Homeland, CIA, NSA, and whatever other departments would want to get involved with what seemed to be shaping into an international charade (if Ivan's theory was correct, which the KGB photo seemed to indicate). No, he wouldn't sit still, couldn't. He wasn't sure what he would do, but certainly not nothing.

His incapacity to understand Stacey's involvement with these Anna and Vadim people had him at a loss, and he figured that side of things would be best left to the feds. Maybe Stacey wasn't involved at all; maybe the letters were Viktoriya's. Maybe Stacey had gotten the books from her, all this going back to Viktoriya in Russia, Anna and Vadim being old friends from the Motherland. But if that were so, Stacey hadn't thought to mention it when the topic came up. And were the Pearson books even old enough to be Viktoriya's? Not that they had to be from Russia, but if not, then...who knew?

Hopefully, the FBI.

He called Ivan. He wanted to know what his friend had held back before. But of course, he didn't answer. He swore under his breath and stood. He couldn't sit there any longer. He went to the register and paid the bill. As he stepped into the parking lot, he observed the veiled position of the sun. It was getting close to six o'clock. It had been a long day so far. He considered going to a bar. If he had to waste time, he might as well be unconscious for it.

A familiar ringtone cut the dreary atmosphere before he could step off the curb.

"Yeah?"

It was Donny.

Jack asked if he could stay with him for a little while, until things began sorting themselves out.

Donny said he'd be home in half an hour.

DONNY HAD NO WIFE, kids, or pets to share his house with, just a girlfriend of three months. So, "*Mi casa, su casa,*" he'd declared upon welcoming Jack through his front door. And from every indication, he'd meant it.

"So, you gonna fill me in now?" Donny asked. It was pushing ten o'clock, and they were sitting on couches opposite each other. They each had a bottle in hand.

Unable to avoid it any longer, Jack finally went through the whole ridiculous story again, pausing only to lift the bottle to his lips and brush away an occasional tear.

Donny sat open-mouthed, staring at his friend. "The FSB?" he repeated. "*Ivan* said that?"

Jack nodded. He'd introduced Ivan to Donny a couple years of ago at a barbecue he and Stacey had hosted.

"I wonder why he isn't calling you back," Donny wondered aloud, his eyes drifting. Then they snapped back to Jack.

"Hey, I'm sorry about the picture thing. I couldn't do anything with it."

"It's fine."

"Can't believe the guy was KGB. What do you think Stacey was doing with it?"

"That's the million-dollar question, isn't it?" After a few seconds passed in silence, he stated, "I can't just sit here and wait, Don. I need to do something."

"Then go to the gym. Hit the bag all night if you need to, but you can't go off playing Charles Bronson with this stuff. And like it or not, you're going to be a suspect."

"That's absurd."

"Is it? *You* were the last one seen with her. Your mother-in-law and son are gone. Your house was burned to the ground—"

"You forgot the part where I threw myself into the ocean, too."

"Says you."

"There are thousands of passengers who—"

"—were asleep. And if there's no video, then all anyone has is your word."

"They turned the ship around. They pulled me out of the water."

Don leaned forward. "And you think the cabin boys are gonna rise to your defense after the cruise line did everything it could to sweep the whole thing under the carpet?"

Jack swore under his breath.

"It would never hold up, of course," Donny concluded, waving his hand in dismissal while leaning back into the couch cushions. "But there's enough initial suspicion to hold you if they wanted to. Be smart. This ain't Hollywood. You can't just go kicking down doors. You'll either get killed or arrested, and either way it'd be the end of a very disappointing and short movie."

Jack stared into the opening of the beer bottle, his mind suddenly churning in another direction. "I just don't understand why she'd keep it a secret from me."

"The letters and stuff? Some secrets are dangerous, Jack. Who knows, maybe she was protecting you. Protecting Joseph."

He sighed and rubbed his eyes. "Viktoriya got us on the boat."

Donny nodded. "Something to think about."

Jack started laughing. "I know she never liked me. You think she could've hired hit men to get rid of me? That she took Joe away from the house before it was burnt down?"

Donny fell silent.

"I'm joking," Jack said.

But Donny didn't seem amused. "The guy was *ordered* to get some of her things before burning down the house..."

Jack stopped laughing. He'd already assumed this, but there was something more in Donny's eyes. "What are you saying?"

"How much didn't she like you?"

"Are you serious?"

"What if Viktoriya did pay someone off to conjure up the cancer story? To get you on the boat? To get rid of you?"

Jack frowned, started to say something, stopped, started again, and ultimately just took another drink.

The Russian countess...

Donny continued, "She moved, for god's sake. Took your son somewhere. Why the hell would she do that?"

Could it be true? Jack thought. Could his mother-in-law hate him that much? Would she have the resources to pull it off? The black-and-white photo of the man came marching into his mind's eye, posing in the form of some vague answer spelled out with three single letters.

K-G-B.

He ran an unsteady hand through his hair. "The guy I shot...he was surprised to see me. And not in an 'I didn't think you were home' sort of way. I wasn't supposed to be there."

"That's because you were supposed to be dead. That's the thing, Jack. If you disappear out in the ocean, this story's over. Someone gets away with it, no questions asked. But now here you are asking questions, getting the FBI involved. Hell, you're connecting dots that no one would've thought twice about. You're shooting the people who are trying to clean it up." He put the bottle to his mouth, letting Jack ponder his words.

Jack looked down at his feet. "If you're right, if this all goes back to Viktoriya and has nothing to do with the books or letters or the FSB—" He stopped, unable to actually suggest it.

Donny chewed his lip for a second. "Do I think Stacey could be in on it?"

Jack looked up, his eyes submerged beneath fresh domes of water.

A phone rang and startled them both.

Jack stood and began tossing cushions, looking for his cell. When he found it, he saw Ivan's name on the screen. "Ivan?" he answered. He walked out of the room, leaving Donny behind. "Tell me what you're not telling me. I know there's something in those letters that—"

Before Jack could cross the threshold into another room, he froze.

"What do you mean?" he whispered, his voice trembling.

Donny looked up.

Jack felt the floor beneath his feet start to move, and he stumbled sideways, leaning against the wall for support.

"You okay, Jack?" Donny got up and stepped toward him.

"Thanks," he whispered into the phone. Then he hung up. Turning to face Donny, he said, "I think I'm gonna need something stronger to drink."

"What is it? What's wrong?"

"Ivan thinks that the Anna in the letters...is Stacey."

20

HE WOKE UP FROM the dream to discover that he'd fallen off the couch. The dream—unreachable moonlight shimmering through depths of liquid darkness—lingered for a while after, and relief didn't erase the feeling of abandonment until he was back on the couch and listening to the *tick-tick-tick* of the wall clock hanging on a nearby wall. Each second helped escort him to the present and back into Donny's house. Five minutes later, the nightmare was replaced by facts just as terrible. And the tears began to fall again.

DONNY CAME DOWN THE stairs and passed through the morning light that was streaming through the dining room window. He was dressed in shorts and a T-shirt that was fading badly around an NFL shield.

"Hungry?" he asked Jack. He disappeared into the kitchen.

Jack was still on the couch, staring into the mysteries of life as seen woven into the throw rug beneath his feet. "No," he muttered.

"You have to eat," Donny called back.

"Don't you have to work?" Jack dropped his head and grabbed handfuls of his hair.

"It's Saturday."

Saturday. *It's been a whole week?* Jack forced himself to his feet and padded into the kitchen. In some ways, it felt like seven years had gone by and, in others, just seven hours. "Cops don't work on the weekends?"

"Not this one." Donny got some coffee brewing. "When are you supposed to go back?"

Jack didn't think he could ever go back. "The cruise was supposed to last another week." He didn't want to think about work. Or whatever would have to be done about his house. He didn't care. Not right now. Not in light of Ivan's revelation. That Anna was Stacey.

He sat at the table and stared out into the morning, watching little birds dart around the bushes surrounding the small patio out back. What was it that the Bible said? Something about not worrying for your life, what you'll eat, drink, or wear? That the birds don't gather more than they need day to day, and yet God takes care of them? But he'd seen birds fly into plate-glass windows before.

He sighed. *God...* Stacey didn't believe in God. He always wondered how she could be so sure that everything existed by dumb luck, that nothing had any meaning beyond whatever some evolved feelings had decided to trick us into believing... But if life was an accident with no purpose or value and the human race wasn't any better than the rest of the animal kingdom, then no one had the right to hold anyone else accountable for anything.

He knew some said that the concept of God was a product of human evolution, the morality-maker that enabled a greater chance of survival for the greatest species. But there were two things wrong with that. First, if they believed that devotion to a God was seen fit by the evolution they espoused, why then reject it? In rejecting it (at least this was how he saw it, anyway), they were rejecting the wisdom of their own god. It didn't make sense. And second, to believe that natural selection and evolution deemed it necessary to trick mankind into believing in some deity so as to prolong its existence via moral barriers would be attributing some form of self-consciousness to evolution, making it the god they didn't believe in.

But even if it was the way they said, it was still pointless in the end. What did it matter that people tried killing him, or that Stalin killed sixty million people? It was just survival of the fittest. And there was no justice or fairness in that.

He thought of Grandmom's smiling face and the worn Bible held tight in her feeble grasp. Then he broke his eyes away from the care-free play of the birds and tried to chase away all the near-death musings from his mind.

Maybe he did drown. Maybe the thoughts of the afterlife were due to the fact that he was *in* the afterlife.

"Maybe I'm dead," he said. And for a second, Jack thought that Donny might just fizzle away, disappear back into the imagination of purgatory once he'd figured it out. The jig was up, he'd cracked the code, the first part of the test passed.

But Donny didn't disappear behind a proud smile. Instead, he set two mugs on the counter beside the percolating coffee maker and stared at him. "Are you saying that I'm not real? Because if that's what you're suggesting, I might have to ask you to leave." Then he leaned against the counter and sighed. "I know that all of this has to be taking a toll on you. Everything's happening so fast, it has to be messing with your head, the world spinning out of control. But you're not dead. You're not asleep in some government lab. You're not on an alien spacecraft. You're in my house. Come on, man. Get it together." He turned to the stove.

"If Stacey is the Anna in the letters..." The possibilities had circled around his head all night, but he'd refrained from reaching out for them. Like planets he knew to be there but not wanting to observe them with a telescope for fear of finding out that, yes, mankind actually was the product of a genetic experiment conducted by green men on Mars. Actually examining any of the insinuations could have sent him over the edge last night, but he knew that he'd have to face them eventually. He decided that eventually would be now.

"The way I see it," Donny said, filling the two porcelain mugs, "is that either she had her mother set all this up to be with Vadim again, which would mean that she knew she didn't have cancer; she thought she had cancer, and Viktoriya helped Vadim get her back unbeknownst to Stacey; or this has nothing to do with a past love relationship, and it's all strictly business." He handed a blue Fraternal Order of Police mug to Jack. "KGB-type business."

"You think Stacey—"

"—*Anna*."

"Maybe."

"Possibly."

"You think that my wife could be a Russian spy?"

Donny shrugged. "I'm a detective. I'm trained to consider every possibility. Granted, it's not the most likely one, but —"

"But until we find out who the man in the photo is, who Vadim is, what Viktoriya's up to, why they wanted me dead, whether or not Stacey's alive..."

"Yeah, we don't know much of anything, Jack. So here's my advice: stop thinking about it. You're only driving yourself crazy. You don't know. Don't go throwing your marriage away or disrespecting Stacey's memory until you have all the facts."

Seeing his own face move back and forth in his coffee, he asked, "Is that what you'd do?"

"Hell no. But I'm telling you what *you* should do. Wait. Keep your head down. Stay alive. Let the feds figure this thing out. You ain't gonna help anyone by getting yourself killed or locked up."

He lifted the cup and took a sip. "Fine."

"Good. Now, I mean it. Don't go dumping on Stacey until you have a reason in stone. She's your soul mate, your son's mother, and my friend. Give her the benefit of the doubt."

"'Love hopes all things, believes all things...'" he muttered.

"What's that?"

Jack looked up. "Something from the Bible."

"Didn't know you still remembered all that stuff."

"Neither did I." He took another sip. But the verse hadn't come from school; it had come from the wall of Grandmom's living room.

Memories came flooding back. Memories of Jack catching her standing there, tears in her eyes, just staring at the framed words, as if God's hand had taken to scribbling on walls again. He could recall every detail of those moments, her black shoes over pantyhose, the flowered dresses she loved to wear, her glasses hanging from her neck, the whirl of white hair crowning her head... She had never explained what it was that made that specific scripture so special to her, but Jack knew it had to do with Grandpa.

The story was that he'd died of a heart attack on his way to the train after work one day. But what was usually omitted from the story was where he was coming from. He had surely died after work, but he had not been coming straight from work. And when five hundred dollars was found in his pocket, the rumors began to circulate. Prostitutes, cocaine, you name it. Of course, Grandmom always rejected such nonsense, even if she couldn't explain it herself. Their marriage had been a good one, and she wasn't about to let some mysterious unknown tarnish the whole thing. Yeah, it was Grandpa's death that made those verses special to her, Jack was pretty certain of that; especially now that they seemed applicable to his own situation.

"You mind if I take a shower?" he asked Donny.

"I'm making us breakfast, man. Relax for a second." He opened the fridge and took out a carton of eggs. "When we're done eating, you can take a shower. God knows you need one. You smell like pickled diarrhea."

And he realized that his last shower had been shared with Stacey.

Or Anna...

JACK STEPPED INTO THE hallway with a bath towel tied around his waist and called out for Donny. When Donny didn't answer, Jack assumed he was still out on his morning jog through the neighborhood. He went into Donny's bedroom and, opening dresser drawers, began looking for some clean clothes that might fit him. Jack was a respectable one-eighty-five with a six-pack, but it wasn't because Donny was a donut cop on the verge of a heart attack that Jack would most likely be unable to fit into his clothes. Donny was two hundred and twenty pounds of solid, veins-popping-out mass. And he never ate donuts.

Movement in his periphery put his search on pause. Standing tall, he turned and gazed into a full-length mirror that was hanging on the wall across from him. He didn't look one-eighty-five anymore. He looked frail, weak. A salesman. And he wondered just how in the world this small man staring back at him was going to set things right.

With a gun, that's how. Guns were the great equalizers, as the man in his garage had learned. But then, that was what Donny and Johnson were talking about, wasn't it? That was the kind of Hollywood crap that would get him killed. *Or save his life*, as had been the case with the intruder. With nowhere to go, though, it was irrelevant. He could daydream all he wanted of storming some Communist compound with his 9 mm blazing, rescuing his wife and son from the hands of some ridiculous James Bond villain with metal teeth, but without a compound to storm, the fantasy could never even tempt becoming a reality.

He turned away from the sight and went back to the dressers, rummaging through socks and...black-laced lingerie? Unless his friend was into some really strange stuff or spent his undercover nights in drag, it looked as if Donny's girlfriend had begun to take over ample dresser space. He found three more outfits, some T-shirts, pajamas, and some really short jean shorts that he hoped were hers, too. But that didn't seem like something Donny would allow. Sharing his bed with a woman was one thing, but his dresser? That wasn't the Donny he knew. Maybe this relationship was serious. If so, it would be the first for his friend.

Setting down the lace and pushing from his mind the more recent memories that it suggested, he settled on the smallest clothes he could find. A dark pair of jeans that fit him fine and a tight black T-shirt that was probably the girlfriend's. He pulled them on and looked in the mirror. The shirt was a little tight, but it made him look more like the one-eighty-five he used to be. He just double-checked to make sure there was no Victoria Secret branding hidden anywhere.

When he turned back to close the drawers, he noticed a little black box nestled in the corner of the top drawer. Curious, he took it out and flipped open the lid. A diamond ring. It was serious. Jack couldn't believe it. He put the box back before Donny could walk in behind him and catch him in his girlfriend's clothes holding the engagement ring, all his dresser drawers opened. That would be awkward. Jack grabbed a pair of socks, shut the drawers, and went back to the bathroom for his sneakers.

Finally clean and dressed for the first time in a week, he descended the stairs. And though the fresh feeling didn't do anything for the nightmare decor still hanging in his soul, it did fill him with an eagerness to get something done. But without direction, he could only settle down on the patio and sit beneath the ascending sun, thinking.

He thought about *The House of Thunder* by Dean Koontz, *October's Ghost* by Ryne Douglas Pearson, *Seventeen Moments of Spring* by Yulian Semyonov... They were all novels of Soviet interest, but each one was as different as the next.

He hadn't seen a note in Pearson's *Simple Simon*, though he supposed he could've missed it. But if the notes were pertinent to the reason why the books were being removed from his house, either to save them from the fire or to ensure their destruction via another means, then *Simple Simon* might have been left behind because it didn't share the same relevance as the others. Or the man hadn't found it in the midst of the clothes piled on the bed. Unless, believing Jack to be dead and knowing that Stacey had *Simple Simon* on the boat with her, he would have no reason to look for it. How the guy would know that, though, was way beyond him.

If only he could examine the novel again, but holding his hand up in the air and having the morning breeze reassemble it in his grasp was probably just as likely as finding the paperback still intact beneath the smoldering pile of his former home.

He went back inside and sat himself at Donny's computer. A screensaver was going through a slideshow of bikini-clad beauties positioned erotically in front of various world-renowned locations. The Giza Plateau, Easter Island, Mount Rushmore, the Great Wall of China. As Jack chased the airbrushed and silicone-loaded hotties away with a gentle move of the mouse, he wondered if married life would finally mature Donny.

He entered *Simple Simon* into Amazon's search bar. Though he didn't think *Mercury Rising* involved a Soviet plot, he wanted to make sure that the movie was true to the novel in that regard. After reading through a few reviews, it seemed that it was. One reviewer stated, "The NSA side of the story made it a great techno-thriller. The government conspiracy was so believable that I wouldn't be surprised to find similar things being discussed on C-Span. Now that I know what to look for..." It sounded like Jack's type of story. Like Stacey's.

But the thing that was odd about Stacey having this novel (apart from it being in the same series with *October's Ghost*) was that she'd been getting all her books from the library lately. So why had she paid for this particular one? If it was sent to her like the others had been, then it would be part of the same puzzle whether it had a Soviet plot or not.

And then, depending on what I believed was going on, I'd either want my wife back or I wouldn't...

Was Johnson actually hinting at...

The screensaver came back on, the near-naked women smiling at him, promising things they could never offer. *Would* never offer. They were teasing him. But fake or not, they were beautiful. Though not as beautiful as Stacey. And she had made him an actual promise. Made a covenant with him. The looks of seduction she teased him with actually led to fulfillment. And again, the God thoughts crept back into his thought process, beauty one of the reasons he rejected atheism. He couldn't believe that beauty was an accident, that virtues like truth and love weren't virtues at all but just strange quirks fabricated by chance to simply confuse a pointless reality. And then this splinter of doubt came infecting his conviction: what if she had been *too* perfect? She could have certainly done better than him. What if this Vadim guy was—

A sudden thought came crashing through his psyche like a thunderbolt from Olympus, riding the wings of a memory. A memory from that night on the boat. Of what Stacey had said to him from beneath the depths of a drunken stupor.

I haven't gotten this drunk since Joseph was conceived!

To which he replied, "What are you talking about? You were as sober as a judge..."

That must've been the other guy, then!

He took a deep breath, refusing to accept that line of thought, focusing on Grandmom's picture. *Love believes all things, hopes all things.* He wouldn't throw away the validity of their relationship on idiotic conjecture.

He just wouldn't.

He walked out to the patio.

21

HE OPENED HIS EYES, and the first thing he noticed was the sun's changed position in the sky. It was now above the big puffy clouds and the chem trails cutting paths through them. He squinted against the brightness and lifted his head off the back of the chair, absorbing his surroundings. After the mental re-entry back to his current location, he forced himself to his feet and walked to the kitchen. The microwave displayed 12:22. He'd been asleep for almost three hours. "Don?" he called.

A knock came from the front door.

"Hey, Don?" he hollered again, drifting to the door. But Donny didn't answer, and a cold finger of worry began tracing his spine. He knew Donny was in great shape, but even he wouldn't just take off on a random three-hour run. He put an eye to the peephole.

And there Agent Johnson stood, impatiently looking up and down the street as if he didn't want to be seen by the ice-cream truck approaching from the next street over, some obnoxious jingle trying to pull kids from their video games.

Jack opened the door. "Hey."

Johnson walked past him without reciprocating the greeting.

"Are you looking for me or Don? Because I'm not sure where he is. He went for a jog, and I fell asleep out on the patio—"

"Let's go," Johnson commanded, not waiting for Jack to finish. His face was pulled tight with stress.

Jack shook his head, confused. "What do you mean? Where?"

"Just get whatever you need, and let's go." There was no flexibility in his voice.

Jack hesitated.

"Go, damn it!" Johnson shoved him.

"All right," he mumbled. He went to the couch he'd slept on the night before and reached beneath it. He pulled out the Smith & Wesson and tucked it into the back of his borrowed jeans. When he got back to Johnson, the agent was looking out the window.

"What's going on?" Jack asked.

"Come on." Johnson opened the door and led him to a blue Dodge Intrepid.

"This your car?"

"Just get in."

Minutes later, they were on Broad Street and headed for PA 309.

"Give me your phone," Johnson ordered.

"Why?"

"Just do it."

Jack pulled it out and handed it over. Johnson had the SIM card out in two seconds and then tossed it out the window. Before Jack could protest, Johnson sent the rest of the phone after it. "They shut us down," he stated, not needing to explain to "Jerry" why he would ever throw a cell phone out the window. There was no missing the anxiety in his clipped voice or the way he was nervously glancing at the rearview mirror every five seconds.

"Who?"

"CIA."

Jack paused, the sound of the road passing beneath them a soothing soundtrack at odds with the happenings of their world. "Why?"

"Apparently Vadim has a unique relationship with the Agency."

"What does that mean?"

Johnson stole a quick glance at him while tapping against the steering wheel. "Your wife was born in Russia, 1974. Her real name is Anna Aleksandrov, born to parents Natasha and Dmitri Aleksandrov. Dmitri was the KGB man in the photo. He died in 1982, a couple of years after Natasha left the country with Anna. They were Stacey and Viktoriya by the time they showed up here in New York."

Jack couldn't seem to get his mouth to move.

Johnson continued, "Vadim Sidorov came over in the mid '90s and was activated by the SVR in '98. Whether Anna was aware of that or not, I wasn't able to find out. He and Anna were married in 1999."

Jack's world dropped into an abyss murkier than the one he'd been rescued from a week ago. He just stared at the road flying toward them, not really seeing the cars Johnson was passing. His mind was numb.

"Sorry," Johnson said, acknowledging the information overload. But he went on anyway. "The CIA turned Vadim in '05—the same year Stacey and Viktoriya showed up in Philadelphia. Obviously, the Agency doesn't want other departments sorting through their double agent's laundry. They're protecting his identity and whatever they're planning on using him for."

Jack finally turned his head. But though the news that Stacey had been married before was devastating to *him*, it didn't explain why they were flying north up Broad Street in a car that, judging from the girly magazines littered across the back seat and the stuffed animals positioned against the rear windshield, was not Agent Johnson's personal vehicle.

"What happened?" Jack finally managed to ask.

"Donny's dead."

And the world just kept spiraling away.

"Hit and run this morning."

Shock crushed him. But the size of the revelation was too large to fit through the space of comprehension, and the full weight of the news was postponed until a more opportune time.

"Your friend Ivan is missing, too," he added.

Jack stared ahead, not blinking, not moving, not breathing. And then, as if some invisible restraint was snapped, he exploded into a fit of rage, throwing his fists into the dashboard, swearing with each strike.

When he was finally done striking the car, Jack put his head in his hands and wept.

Johnson waited three miles before interrupting him. "I don't know if this is the CIA or the Russians cleaning up, but you need to lie real low for a while. I'm taking you somewhere you'll be safe. You'll stay there until you hear from me. I know you want to find your son, but right now you need to worry about staying alive."

Jack forced a deep breath. "You think the CIA's cleaning up after Vadim?" He couldn't figure out why the Russians would be knocking people off.

"Remember when the FBI caught those guys who were planning on blowing up a bridge in Cleveland?" Johnson asked.

Jack snorted with disgust. "Yeah, after recruiting and supplying them." He looked over at him and shook his head. "Way to go."

Johnson didn't say anything.

But Jack was angry, and venting with his mouth came naturally when his target was something he couldn't touch with his hands. "They find them, recruit them, train them, supply them, and in some cases even drive the van to the target! Then they bust them at the last second and parade themselves like heroes for the mainstream media. And the public eats it up with praise while handing over all their rights."

Agent Johnson again checked the road behind them. "Look, I know all that. Which is why I brought it up. You're right. Cleveland, Massachusetts, New York, Portland..." He sighed. "It looks like Vadim could be in the middle of a similar situation."

Jack's eyes narrowed. He wiped away a tear. "You mean they're setting him up for something? Or they're keeping their scapegoat from making front-page news before they can pull off a black op?" If the CIA had Vadim pegged as their fall guy for some false-flag operation, then Jack being a "monkey wrench" was a massive understatement, his surviving the dip in the big drink clogging their conspiratorial toilet with something much larger. "You talking some kind of Northwoods thing? To incite a war with Russia?"

Johnson understood the reference, which involved the Joint Chiefs of Staff drawing up plans to commit terrorist acts in the US to garner public support for a war against Cuba, and shook his head. "All I know is that anyone who knows about your wife's previous husband is having a hard time staying alive right now."

The car fell into silence for ten miles. Until Jack started laughing.

"What is so funny?" Johnson asked.

"Operation Ajax is funny."

Johnson looked confused.

"1953, the CIA-led coup on Mossadegh to keep him from nationalizing Iran's oil..."

"I know what it is. Why is it funny?"

"Because it was the closest Iran ever came to being a democracy, and we go in and install the Shah, which led to the rise of Islamic fundamentalism and anti-Americanism in the Middle East. Then we use that fundamentalism by creating and training Al-Qaida to fight the Soviets in Afghanistan..." He laughed some more. "And now, after the Cold War and the collapse of the Soviet Union, here we are fighting an endless war against our own creation while the very ones we created them to defeat have been nursing their wounds in the background, gaining power while waiting for us to suffer the same fate!" He continued laughing at the insanity of it all.

When Johnson didn't respond, Jack looked back out the window. "Problem-reaction-solution, right?" he mumbled, staring into the returning numbness. He saw in the window's reflection Johnson turn toward him. "Create a problem that causes a reaction, the reaction being the people begging for a solution, the solution being the true agenda all along. You think anyone could've foreseen their government burning Jews in ovens? Hitler only had to burn down his own Parliament building and blame it on his enemies in order to incite a wave of blind national patriotism that swept the Nazis to within an arm's length of world domination."

"Now you're suggesting the US government is made up of Nazis?"

"Wouldn't be surprised. Operation Paperclip was hatched by our government, wasn't it? The Tuskegee Experiment. Besides, governments will always be made up of men. And men will always be corruptible. That's why there's a Constitution. And the right to bear arms. And the balance of powers. And the right to assemble. And free speech." And, as if pulled from the rut his mind had rolled into, he stared back at Johnson. "You really think they're plotting another false flag?"

They both understood the term to be derived from the military practice of flying false colors, a ship hanging the flag of its enemy before targeting one of its own, the attack falsely blamed on the attacking flag in order to justify a reaction against the enemy. There were many historical instances on which they could both draw. Nero's burning of Rome, Operation Himmler, the burning of the Reichstag, the KGB bombing their own in order to justify war with Chechnya, the CIA's Operation Ajax in Iran, the USS *Liberty* incident, Operation Gladio, the US's Operation Northwoods, the Gulf of Tonkin incident, the anthrax notes in the wake of 9/11, and so on and so forth. There were countless incidents throughout history, and even more so recently. Whether Johnson would agree with all of the attacks Jack believed to be a false flag or inside job didn't matter; there were enough out of the bag now to make the conversation frighteningly plausible.

But Johnson just shook his head again, not saying a word.

22

JOHNSON PULLED THE DODGE onto a stone path, the path resting partially concealed between the green walls of a dense forest. The canopy above was so impenetrable that long rays of light could be seen poking through small openings. They were somewhere in the mountains. Jack didn't know exactly where. After more than a dozen turns down small streets and uneven back roads, he'd given up keeping track of their location.

The narrow path led to a small cabin, and Johnson pulled up beside it. He flung the door open. "Come on."

Jack stepped out and stretched, kneading his knuckles into the small of his back. "Whose place is this?"

"Friend of a friend of a cousin." He tried the front door. Locked.

"Anyone live here?"

"Not at the moment." He walked around back and tried the other door. It was locked, too.

"You didn't tell anybody we were coming?" Jack asked.

He shook his head. "Not a soul." Walking across the overgrown yard and to a wooden shed that sat nestled against the tree line, he bent over and flipped a rock. When he stood back up, he had a set of keys in his hand. Wiping them off, he walked back to the door and unlocked it.

Jack followed him into the house and found himself standing in a kitchen that obviously hadn't been used in a long time.

"Stay here." And Johnson went to check the rest of the house. When he came back a minute later, Jack was running his finger through the half an inch of dust on the stove. Johnson frowned. "I thought you'd be smarter than that."

Jack withdrew his finger and swept his gaze up to the water-stained ceiling. "Not that anyone'll ever know I was here, right?"

"That's the idea, but still..." He reached into his pocket and withdrew a cell phone. "It's prepaid." He tossed it to him. "Don't use it unless it's an emergency. You only get one call, and I may not be able to drive back out here. Otherwise, I'll call you when I find out what's going on."

Jack scratched an itch on his forehead. "So, I'll be here for a while?"

"Probably."

"What about food?"

"I got stuff in the car." He led Jack back to the Dodge and opened the trunk. A few grocery bags were lined up beside a 12-gauge double-barrel shotgun and boxes of shells. Johnson took the bags out one at a time.

"You know how to work a shotgun?" he asked Jack.

"Yeah. Where'd you get it?"

"It's my uncle's."

"Thanks."

"Stay on top of the prints. There's a box of gloves in one of the bags. Wear them, it'll be easier than trying to remember what you touched. There's a backpack in one of them, too. I didn't have time to load it myself, but you should keep it ready. If you have to run, you won't have time to pack. If anyone shows up, you grab the gun and the bag and you take off into the woods. If you can't get away in time, then...well, if a person doesn't have a key, then they've got no business being here. Shoot first."

"And what do I do once I'm in the woods?"

Johnson shrugged. "Stay alive."

Again, all kinds of movies came playing back in his mind. The only problem was that John Rambo had a legendary background with the Special Forces, and all Jack could boast of was a game-winning touchdown run in high school. "Yeah..." he mumbled. Then he said, "Will you look for Ivan?"

"I'll keep my eyes open, but I need to lie low on this stuff, too. I'm sorry."

Thinking of Ivan led to another thought. "Is it true that the FSB is more ruthless than the KGB?"

"That's the rumor."

"Do you think there's any chance this could be SVR?"

"A chance? I guess. But I don't know why they'd care about Donny and Ivan." Then he looked at his watch and mumbled, "I have to get back. I'll call as soon as I can. I'm sorry about Donny. He was a good friend." For a moment, it seemed Johnson might shed a tear.

Emotion grabbed Jack, too. "He was going to propose," he whispered.

"What do you mean?" But there was a look of unbelief on the agent's face that said he knew exactly what he'd meant.

"Yeah, I found a ring in one of his drawers while I was looking for clean clothes." He pulled at the T-shirt.

Johnson swore under his breath, and a small smile tugged the corner of his mouth a couple of times as a tear did fall. "Donny married..." He laughed a sad laugh. "That I would've liked to see."

Jack grew angrier at the unfairness of it all. "They're going to get away with it, aren't they? Whoever's behind this?"

"They always do."

"It's not right."

"Never is."

Jack stared at the ground. "Do you think my son is alive?"

"If Stacey's involved in some way, then yes, I'm sure he's doing just fine."

"And if she's not?"

"I don't know, Jack."

They stood silent for a while, listening to unseen birds whistle from their branches.

"If I don't call by Saturday..." Johnson finally said. But he didn't finish the thought. Instead, he shrugged and closed the trunk. "If this is CIA, and the attention on Vadim has compromised them, then it's likely the whole thing might blow over."

But even if it did blow over, Jack was unsure of where it would leave him and Stacey, Vadim and Viki. "So I'm just supposed to hide out here until things settle down and—"

"If you want me to drive you back, I will. But where are you going to stay? And what do you think you'd accomplish? You think maybe Joseph is going to call you one day, tell you where he is? We're way past that now, Jack. People are dying. Someone is covering their tracks, and you're the one exposing them. You need to stay out of the picture until I can figure out what's really going on." He walked to the driver's side door and got in. Once seated behind the wheel, he told him, "It can get cold at night up here." He handed him a long black coat.

"Thanks."

"I'll call you."

"What am I supposed to do?" he complained.

"I don't know. Pray." He shut the door.

"Yeah, thanks." And he watched the taillights flicker on and off as Johnson navigated the car away from him.

Thirty seconds later, he was standing alone in the middle of nowhere, a prepaid cell phone in his pocket, a pistol down his pants, a coat hanging over the crook of his arm, and a shotgun and grocery bags lying at his feet. He took in the new environment and wondered how he'd ended up in this place.

IT WAS DARK OUT, and with no watch on his wrist or working clock on the wall, it was the only thing in the world right now that Jack knew for certain. He was positioned by a window in the corner of the room, sitting in an old rocking chair—all its joints reinforced with webbing from some arachnid artist that he hoped died years ago. But he had the loaded shotgun across his lap just in case.

A candle burned atop the makeshift table beside him, its flickering light casting itself in a reflection against the dirty window he was facing. He could see nothing but the dark impression of night beyond it and his own ghostly silhouette dancing in rhythm to the flame. Scratching an itch on his head that may or may not be imagined, he was instantly bothered by the feel of the probing latex. Wearing the gloves reminded him of Jerry Fletcher keeping his coffee in combination-locked thermoses inside a padlocked refrigerator. But it was Johnson that had suggested it, and if the CIA was after him, he figured no precaution was too extreme.

Jack pushed gently off his toes, moving the chair back and forth and filling the empty house with the sound of creaking wood. On the floor next to his feet was the backpack, fully loaded with everything Johnson had left with him. He was ready to run.

Beneath the dripping candle sat the phone, his eyes drawn to its blank face every two minutes, wondering when it might ring. Johnson hadn't left a charger with him—though there was no electricity anyway—so Jack figured he had about three days, maybe four, until the phone died and he was left to come up with a plan of his own. He hoped it wouldn't come to that.

He wasn't sure how much of this being alone in the middle of the mountains he could take. He'd already worn out a dozen scenarios of how Stacey might've disappeared, and he thought he might have a mental breakdown if he didn't give it a rest. Some scenarios had Stacey laughing at him while making love to her KGB husband, while others saw her floating corpse reaching out in a frozen plea for help. Neither extreme had him clicking his heels across the cracked floorboards.

He just wanted to go to sleep. He was so tired. But he was too scared to sleep. So he kept rocking, staring into the window as if an assassin couldn't place a bullet through his eye from half a mile away with him sitting all candlelit in front of the window like he was. And the questions, like buzzing gnats gunning for his eyeballs, kept coming.

Did Stacey know about her cancer or not? Was Viktoriya working with the CIA to set her up or the FSB? Why would they set her up at all? There were more resourceful ways to make someone disappear. Unless it was a private matter, hired thugs helping put Stacey back together with Vadim. Was Stacey SVR like Vadim? Was Viktoriya KGB like her husband? What about the strange text message Stacey got the night it all started? And what about the books? Why had the guy taken them out of the house? If it was just a matter of Stacey hooking back up with her other husband, why the need to eliminate Donny and Ivan? Was the CIA really plotting an inside job with Vadim as their Russian flag? But why would Stacey be involved? And what about the thing she'd said about Joseph?

His mouth was dry, and he desperately wanted one of the six bottles of water Johnson had put in the bag. But he didn't know how long he was going to be here, so he was trying to conserve them.

His eyes suddenly felt heavy, and the room around him began to fade. Before he could summon the willpower to stop the inevitable, he was asleep.

HE AWOKE WITH A start and knew right away that something had jettisoned him from his slumber. He moved his eyes back and forth, letting them adjust while trying to peer through the room's eerie shadows.

Nothing.

He exhaled the breath he was holding and leaned forward in the chair. The old wood groaned loudly beneath him, but no dagger flew at him from another room, no smoke grenade rolled to a stop at his feet, and no masked men came rappelling down from the ceiling. Slowly, he rose to his feet, debating whether or not to blow out the melting candle beside him. He brought the shotgun up instead, slipping his finger over the double trigger, and stepped carefully toward the back of the cabin. He was sure that whatever had awakened him had come from that direction.

He paused briefly before slipping into the darkness of the kitchen, moving softly to the back door.

And that was when he heard it.

He swore under his breath as perspiration beaded across his forehead. He raised the shotgun.

There it was again. It was coming from outside.

He took a deep breath, worked the doorknob with his latex fingers, and stepped outside. He swung the gun to the left. To the right.

Nothing.

He continued stepping away from the cabin and closer to a pinch of moonlight that was lingering above the ground in the center of the backyard.

Snap.

He jumped, almost squeezing the trigger, and spun around. Something was there, at the edge of the woods by an old toolshed... He was about to call out when a low moan lifted from the ground behind him and brought all the hair on the back of his neck standing to attention. But just before turning to discover the source of the sound, the thing in front of him stumbled out into the moonlight.

Uh-oh.

Jack knew what was behind him even as it exhaled a puff of air from its nostrils—so close that he felt its whispering surge stroke his skin. Forcing his feet to move, he turned around as slowly as he could.

Sniffing the air five yards away was a big black bear.

Jack moved the barrel of the shotgun around so that it was pointing at the beast, and with all the self-control he could muster, made himself take one small step backward at a time. If the cub, now behind him and playing in the silver spotlight, came any closer, then mamma bear might just feel the need to defend her family. Jack had seen footage of bear attacks and wanted no part in the experience.

He made it to the door without the bear taking issue, and slipped inside. Then he went and moved the rocking chair, candle, and backpack into the kitchen. He settled down to keep an eye on the four-legged neighbors. He couldn't avoid the symbology though and again was pestered by thoughts of dreaming.

A bear. *Russia.*

But he would stick with the theory that this was a normal occurrence, that bears lived in the mountains. At least until it stood on its hind legs, reached into its fur, and extracted an AK-47. Once that happened, he would have to face the more unpleasant theories of what was happening and where he truly was.

But by the time he dozed off again, the bear hadn't yet whispered any Russian codes to the cub, pulled out a Pearson novel, or waltzed with his wife through the moonlit clearing.

23

THE CABIN HAD BECOME too claustrophobic for him, so when he woke up and found the bear family gone, Jack decided to take a stroll through the sunlit paths in the woods. He found that the cool morning air, carrying the fresh scent of nature bathed in dew, actually relieved the tension in his gut. But the scene couldn't transport him completely from his trouble, and he kept checking and rechecking the cell phone, making sure he had two bars of reception at all times.

He came to a wide lake that was entertaining a lonely picnic table, its legs strangled by long weeds. He set the shotgun and backpack down across its warped surface and sat down on the bench. He cast his gaze out over the lake.

The sun was sparkling off the smooth water, and there was a mysterious serenity to it all. Until sudden thoughts of Donny came rowing toward him, his high school friend now dead. He tried dodging the painful realization, but the light breeze that was pushing ripples into the lake also seemed to fill the sails of his mind, nudging it into the greater depths of memory's disjointed sea. And it was there that he sank into an odd, incoherent interpretation—death and loss the two lenses of his goggles translating his submerged memories.

An eagle appeared gliding over the water's surface. Its talons dipped beneath the lake and snatched itself a wiggling snack. Just like that. The fish swimming along with its fish-family one second and impaled by razor-sharp claws and flying through the air the next...never to see his gilled kind again, destined only to suffocate and bleed in its unfortunate role in the food chain. And then nothing. Nonexistence. Because wasn't there something in Revelations about no sea in heaven? That would mean no fish, then, right? Unless their resurrected bodies came with wings, and all eternal fish were flying fish. But fish fins strumming golden harps in the clouds just didn't seem right. So the fish then had been destined to a pointless existence and doomed to an excruciating departure into nothingness...

Sure, you could sing a Disney song about the circle of life to make you feel better, but at the end of the day, the circle itself was just a bad carousel ride going nowhere for no reason. But then, if Stacey was right in her theology-absent worldview, *he* was in the same predicament as that fish.

He unzipped the bag and took out a bottle of water and a can of tuna fish. Tuna fish. He laughed at the irony of it. There was a can opener and some plastic utensils that Johnson had included, and once Jack had the lid off the can and its water drained into the dirt at his feet, he began shoveling mouthfuls of warm fish into his mouth. As he forced it down, he watched the eagle disappear over the tree line. Then he looked down at the meat hanging on his plastic fork and asked himself, *Are we all fish?* And he wondered if a can of dolphin safe tuna was going to be the tipping point of his sanity.

He watched the light show over the water and moved his thoughts back to the people who wanted him dead. He wished he knew why. And who. It was true that certain of his views would've gotten him a secret file with the FBI back in Hoover's day, but while he was vocal about his beliefs and most of his friends knew he was a "conspiracy nut," he wasn't any type of activist. He wasn't holding rallies and signing petitions. There was no reason the government of the United States, even the corrupt shadow figures sitting behind the scenes, would think of him as any type of threat. Right? Even if the "threat of terrorism" that was actually threatening the Constitution, allowing intelligence agencies to spy on everyone, did land him on someone's list, there was no way the government would go through all this trouble just because he questioned the official story of...well, everything.

Whoever was after him now was trying to tie off a loose end. But why the initial trouble of tossing him overboard? The answer depended on who "they" were. The cruise would be a convenient way for anyone to get rid of him, but then Stacey's suicide note...that would ensure *her* a new life somewhere. Maybe with Vadim.

Love hopes all things, believes all things...

But if he was in the middle of some false-flag setup, like Johnson had hinted, then maybe the FBI man was right. Maybe all this unplanned attention due to his surviving the fall would derail whatever plan was being concocted. How many people could they afford to take out before the corpses began demanding questions of their own?

Jack washed the remainder of the tuna fish down with another gulp of water. Then, in frustration, he screamed into the woods around him. "Are you out there? Are you watching me?"

But only a few startled squirrels responded by darting up a nearby tree.

He put the gun back down and rested the cell phone on the table next to it, staring. Waiting.

Come on, Johnson.

THE SUN WAS SETTLING comfortably into its afternoon pose by the time he made it back to the cabin. After searching each room for any sign of an intruder, he set the shotgun against the wall and slipped the pack off his shoulders. He unscrewed the cap to his second bottle of water and took a short sip. He stared out the window. Rubbed sweat from his forehead with the back of his hand.

The cell phone rang.

The ringtone was halfway through its third segment by the time he had it out of his pants and up to his ear.

"Hello?"

"It's me," Johnson said.

Jack waited in silence for whatever Johnson had to say, knowing that it would most likely define the rest of his life.

"I've been reassigned to Arizona."

Jack swore under his breath, and he felt what little hope he had tucked away start to crumble.

"Listen," Johnson went on, *"I know where she is."*

"Stacey?" Hope hung on.

"She's in Connecticut."

"With Viktoriya?"

"I don't know where Viktoriya or Joseph is, but it'd be my guess."

Jack's heart struck up a fierce baseline in his chest.

"She's with the other man," Johnson said.

"With—"

"Yes. No more names. Whatever this was going to be is over now. I think you're safe."

"What about—"

"I'll text you the address. That's all I can do now. I'm sorry. Good luck."

The call ended.

Before Jack could even compute what had just happened, the phone beeped, and a text message appeared. An address in Avon, Connecticut, followed by: BE SMART. LOSE PHONE.

And Jack knew where his wife was. That she was alive.

Elation. Fury. Happiness. Jealousy. He was going to get her back. He was going to kill her. He was going to rescue her. He was going to beat the truth out of her. He was going to tell her that everything would be okay...

He picked up the bag and flipped it upside down, spilling its contents onto the floor. Then he selected the items he would need: the gloves, all the water bottles, and the coat. Hoping that Johnson was right about no one coming for him now, he just left the other things on the floor, no longer caring to keep his presence here a secret. With the shotgun in hand, he left the house for the shed, where he found a dull hacksaw. Five minutes and a pair of sore arms later, the shotgun's barrel was trimmed short enough to fit inside the backpack. Ten minutes after that, he was on his way, following the long driveway out to the road.

At the end of the driveway, he reached the gravel road and debated on which way to go. Sweat was already dripping down his face. Right was the way they'd come, and he could only remember a tangled mess of smaller roads that he would never be able to retrace. He went left, figuring there was something just as likely to be up around the bend as not.

But the bend turned into a long straight shot of gravel cut through more mountain. Jack was no woodsman; he was a salesman from Philly. He loved taking Joseph on fishing trips to the lake and hikes through the state park, but he'd always preferred the surf to bears and snakes. So as he walked along, he couldn't help but keep a wary eye on the sea of green waving at him.

The pack was heavy, and the straps were beginning to dig into his shoulders. It was pushing three o' clock, and the day's heat seemed to reach its maximum yield, making the walk much more uncomfortable. Gravel moved beneath his feet, trying to fling him onto his face as he pressed up an incline. But at least the challenge of it forced him to concentrate on the exercise rather than the implications parading behind the news of Stacey being alive in Connecticut with Vadim.

An hour later, dripping with sweat, Jack stepped onto a blacktop road that was split in half by a white stripe—another step closer to civilization.

The road stretched past him, going left to right, and his tired legs chose the downhill route. But right away he noticed a difference in the temperature. The gravel road had been covered by the forest canopy, but the blacktop had no such roof, the power cables slithering through the air from one pole to the next. The sun had beaten its heat into the asphalt all day long, and now he was walking over an oven as well as beneath one. He swung the pack off his back and let it fall to the ground. He took out a bottle of warm water. It tasted like plastic, but he figured anything would be better than having to drink his own urine—which he'd heard survivalists advocate in severe situations.

He massaged his aching shoulders and tried resisting the urge to sit for a few minutes. *Keep going,* he told himself. Thoughts of Joseph and all the memories still needing to be created pushed him on. Whether or not Stacey (or *Anna)* would be a part of his future, Joseph certainly would be. He would make sure of that.

He swatted at her drunken remark as it came back to sting him once more. *Love believes all things, hopes all things...*

24

AT THE BOTTOM OF the blessed hill, the road joined another via a red, octagonal sign that read STOP in white letters—yet another sign of civilization. Though a traffic light would have been preferred, beggars couldn't be choosey, could they? And Jack walked on.

Half an hour later, he was standing in front of a parking lot encircling what could have been Atlantis itself as far as he was concerned. Ma's. It was a local, backwoods-type restaurant, but as long as it was operated by people and not apron-wearing raccoons, he was all for it.

Standing next to Ma's was a supply store and gas station. And if the restaurant was Atlantis, then its neighbor must be Asgard, Mu, Bensalem, Olympus,

Mount Zion, or Ararat. He didn't prefer one to the other, and he could have dropped to his knees in praise of any one of their rulers. If not for the fact that he blamed such deities for the mess he was in to begin with. If the old mythology contained even a whisper of truth in its presentation of the gods—that they were up there entertaining themselves on human misery—then Jack would...well, he didn't know what he could do other than curse at them. Thrusting a finger to the heavens in defiance of some trident-wielding, bearded god adorned in a dress did offer some satisfaction, but not nearly enough.

There was, however, the monotheistic God that his early schooling had taught him about, a God he was less anxious to cast expletives at. Father Jacob had lectured about a God that, for some reason or another, allowed pain and misery in order that such things as joy, love, and worth could actually be realized and appreciated, that man would be forced to deal with the reality of his eternal soul. Free will required contrasts. Good and evil. Light and darkness. Misery and hope. But Jack didn't know about any of that. Though if the Man Upstairs could rectify his situation, then maybe he'd make it a point to revisit those uncomfortable pews he'd hated sitting in. Maybe. If he lost everything, then there would be nothing left to appreciate, and God could take His free will and—

The direction of the breeze shifted, and the glorious smell of bacon erased every other thought. There was pig to be eaten.

As he approached the front door, he noticed that the screen was torn in a few places, the wood framing it old and splintered, paint faded and chipped. But the sweet aroma of pig being burnt on the altars of Ma's Atlantis carried him through the door like one of those old cartoons, his toes wiggling above the ground. He didn't even look behind him to make sure this wasn't some sort of trap, armies of black SVR bears closing on his location.

"Hi there," came a girl's voice.

But Jack's eyes hadn't yet adjusted to the darker interior of the restaurant. "Ma?" he asked.

Then a young girl, probably in her late teens, stepped forward and into the light pouring through the screen door behind him. She smiled, the flannel shirt she was wearing rolled up to her elbows, an apron covering her faded jeans, her dark hair in pigtails.

"If by 'Ma' you mean Ma's great-granddaughter, then yes, that's me," she said through an innocent smile. She looked him up and down. "You look like you could use a glass of water, mister."

"Do you have ice?"

She laughed. "Go grab a seat, and I'll get ya the tallest glass we have."

"Thanks." He stepped into the belly of the place. There were picnic tables set up along the windows on the street side and smaller tables against the other. He counted six customers, and none looked like they'd just come from the former Soviet Union. Though, without a red star stamped to a big fur-laced hat, he wasn't exactly sure how he'd be able to tell.

He took a seat by the window and tried to ignore the inquisitive glances he was getting from the small gathering of local diners. He set the backpack on the bench and against the wall beside him. Then he took out his wallet and counted out his cash. He wasn't going to use a credit card, though he was pretty sure a place like this wouldn't accept them anyway. No doubt a terrorist organization for sure. *Ma's—yummy, homegrown terrorism since 1890. Cash only.*

The girl walked over and set a tall glass of ice water down on the table in front of him. The glass was sweating, hundreds of water drops sliding down and gathering in a ring around its base. It looked to Jack like it had been scooped from the Fountain of Youth itself, and he wondered if there really was a halo around it.

"You're not related to Ponce de Leon, are you?" If it was scooped from such a place and Ma had inherited the secret location from her ancestors, the drink might cost more than he had.

A look of confusion crossed her face.

"Never mind."

"Would you like something to eat?" she asked instead.

"Uh..." He looked around for a menu.

She smiled again. "You ain't from around here, are you? What would you like?"

He shrugged, and his sore shoulders cursed him for it. "You have burgers?"

"You bet. Cheese?"

"Please."

"Okeydokey." She spun away.

When he went to pick up the dripping glass, it almost slipped right through his fingers. If it had, he would've licked the puddle up off the picnic table, broken glass, splinters and all. The ice-cold well water coated his throat and splashed into his stomach to a chorus of singing angels.

Ten minutes later, the young girl was back and sliding a huge plate toward him. The burger was the biggest he'd ever seen, and it was buried beneath a mountain of fries. He could make out a sliver of green canoe beneath the salty crosshatching and knew it must be a pickle.

"Wow," he said.

"I'll get you another glass of water." She took the empty glass away.

Once he finished the meal, which was beyond earthly description compared to tuna fish straight from the can, he made his way to an old register that Ma could have used a century ago. A guy with a beard stood behind it, waiting for him. The girl's father, no doubt.

"Everything okay, mister?" he asked politely.

"Perfect. What do I owe you?"

"Five bucks."

He'd eaten the equivalent of two fast food "value" meals and was fairly certain this had been real, organic meat. "I'll have to come here more often," he said.

The man smiled and took a five from him. "What brings you up this way? Looks like you walked from wherever it is you came from." There was just a hint of suspicion hidden in his voice.

"I was staying at a cabin for a couple of days. Must've left the interior lights on in the car, 'cause now the battery's dead. And of course my phone died. And I forgot my charger..."

The handwritten sign on the wall behind him that was advertising raw milk told Jack that he could be carrying an M-16 and this guy probably wouldn't care.

"Isn't that stuff illegal?" Jack asked, nodding to the poster.

The man laughed and pulled a revolver from beneath the counter. "The FDA comes in here, and they'll be in for a surprise."

Yup, terrorist.

Raw milk was the new plutonium.

"If I get some gun-toting FDA bureaucrat showing up here without reasonable cause, a warrant or nothin', I'm gonna exercise my constitutional right and tell him to get the heck off my property."

"Amen," Jack said, though he knew that pulling a gun on a federal officer these days would only get the guy an early special on a pair of pine pajamas.

"The FDA says it's illegal to advertise the health benefits of vitamins and supplements. Such statements are not approved," he put air quotes around the word "approved" and then laughed, waving his hand. "Don't get me started."

"A man after my own heart," Jack replied. But being in the hurry that he was, that was the wrong thing to say. The guy took it as an invitation to continue venting.

The guy leaned forward. "You know what my theory is?"

And Jack nodded his agreement that money and power was the answer behind every head-scratching thing in Washington. From cure-for-profit versus prevention, to the FBI shooting farmers' pigs, to GMOs and the death of farming. He'd covered a lot of ground in five minutes. But five minutes was all Jack was willing to give him, best burger ever made or not. "Well, keep your chin up, and your gun loaded, I guess."

"Yeah, same to you, mister. Not every day you run into someone who knows what's really going on."

Jack slapped the counter. "We tinfoil hats stick together. Take care." He opened the door and stepped back into the parking lot. As he crossed the stone driveway, he wondered if there were a lot of people like him out here. More Jerrys.

Maybe if things didn't turn out well, he'd move out this way. Probably not.

He took his full belly over to the gas station and wasn't surprised to find that it was the type you'd expect to see in a horror movie, the last outpost where the old, decrepit guy in overalls was chewing a long piece of grain and warning you away. But the guy at this gas station wasn't that old or in overalls. When he saw Jack strolling up to the two pumps, he came out of the supply shop to meet him.

"Can I help you?" he asked.

Jack looked around. "I need to get to Connecticut."

The man chuckled as he ran a calloused hand through his unruly hair. "On foot? That'll take you a while."

"Thinking of hitchhiking," he said. "But I'd like to get on the right road."

The man considered him. "The sun's gonna be goin' down soon. I wouldn't recommend walking the roads at night. No streetlights. You'd likely get run over."

"Or shot by a bear." *Had he really just said that?*

The gas station attendant looked at him funny.

Yup.

The guy pressed ahead, uncertain. "I don't think you have to worry about that out here. Maybe in Montana they have bears packin' heat..."

Jack smiled, thinking that he was truly losing his mind. "That's good to know. So which way you think I should be heading?" He squinted up and down the road.

"Well, I guess you'd want to find your way to 84." He sighed, thinking. "Wish I could give you a lift, but..." He waved at the station and shop behind him.

Business was booming. "I appreciate it, but I'm okay walking." Though he wasn't. In fact, he was eyeing the pickup parked behind the supply store. Its windows were down.

"Well, then keep walking down this road until you get to the next. Go right, and just keep walking." He spit on the ground. "I really hope someone picks you up."

"Me too. Thanks." He turned away and headed for the road again.

Once the gas station was out of sight, he left the road and doubled back through the woods, coming up behind the supply store.

He left the woods, crept up to the pickup, and stuck his head through its open window. No key in the ignition, and he was more certain than ever that people only did that in the movies. But he checked beneath the floor mat and above the visor just in case. The gods weren't making this easy.

He snuck away from the only vehicle in the back lot and went to the back door of the shop. It was standing wide open. He could hear music playing from within, the guy he'd met whistling along to the country tune from an unseen position in the front of the store. Zeus in a cowboy hat and flannel? This was definitely not Asgard. Jack stepped into the store, trying to think of any reason he could give the guy if he were to get caught. He couldn't think of one. The back was just a small storage room with an open doorway leading to the rest of the store, and right there, beside the doorway, was a row of hooks—one of which had a set of keys dangling from it.

Jack quietly pulled on a pair of latex gloves from the backpack and crawled to the keys. He slowly wrapped his hands around them and lifted them off their perch without so much as a jingle. Once he was back to the open door, he sorted through the keys until finding one that declared FORD. He slid it off the ring, placed the remainder of the keys on the ground, and headed for the truck.

He opened its faded door and slid the key into the ignition. He placed his backpack on the bench seat and then pulled the gearshift into neutral. He couldn't alert the man to his "borrowing" of the truck right from the get-go or some backwoods sheriff would be pulling him over in minutes, and all hopes of getting to Connecticut would be dashed. After a quick look around, he leaned all his weight against the doorframe and used his aching legs to push the truck forward. Thankfully, it was already facing the road. He just needed the guy's face to stay buried in a fishing magazine and his music loud enough to drown out the rolling tires.

The truck moved. His legs screamed. And twenty yards later, he had the truck turning out onto the road. He braced himself for the blast of a gunshot that would rip through his back and stop all this, but none came. He jumped behind the wheel, knocking the backpack to the floor, and pulled the door closed. As the truck rolled downhill in neutral, it began picking up speed, and soon the supply shop was behind him. The rearview mirror gave no indication that anyone had seen him. He started to breathe again.

At the bottom of the hill, he brought the engine to life.

25

RATHER THAN TAKING 84 all the way to Connecticut, Jack followed signs to Allentown instead. Five minutes into the city, he pulled into a gas station. He paid cash for ten gallons of gas and a Connecticut map after using the bathroom to flush the phone down the toilet. He got directions to the nearest Greyhound from the cashier and was relieved that it wasn't far.

By eight o'clock, he was walking into the station, leaving the pickup behind and trying to soothe his conscience by reassuring himself that the relocation was justified. But by the time he had a ticket to Hartford in his hand, the truck was as good as forgotten, expunged from his thinking by the high tide of his own concerns. Like the wrapped present he was carrying under his arm.

It wasn't worth trying to smuggle the shotgun onto the bus, so he'd put on the coat Johnson packed for him and left the backpack beneath the seat of the truck. Even if Johnson was wrong about this whole thing being over with, he wasn't about to get in a shoot-out with agents while squeezed onto a bus full of innocent civilians.

The pistol, however, was a different story. He couldn't leave that in the truck because it was registered under his name. It wouldn't take any great sleuth to pin the truck's theft on him, which probably wasn't a huge offense, but one that would beg questions he was sure the CIA would much rather remain unanswered. If the CIA, or whoever was behind all this, was willing to forget the whole operation, then Jack didn't want to give them any reason to reconsider. He would go to his grave with his lips sealed if his silence would ensure the safety of his family (though if something did happen to Joseph, or if Stacey was an innocent victim in all this, he would dedicate the rest of his life to shouting his story from the mountaintops). But first, he had to find them, and that meant concealing the pistol in a way that wouldn't raise suspicion.

On his way to Allentown, he'd stopped at a Staples and got all he needed to conceal the Smith & Wesson in a cardboard box, wrapping it with birthday paper. Had the post office been open at that hour, he would've just sent the gun back to his neighbor along with a note. But as it was, he would be glad to have a weapon with him in Avon. He wasn't sure what to expect, and if confronting an SVR-CIA double agent, he would certainly prefer to be armed.

The bus ride to Hartford was just over two hundred miles and would take eight hours. According to the map, he would be dropped off ten miles east of Avon. He could walk that if he needed to. One of the few trips made from Allentown to Hartford during the day was scheduled to leave at 8:55, so he only had to wait half an hour before departing.

By the time he was seated on the bus, the birthday present on the empty seat beside him, he was looking forward to the eight-hour trip. Whatever was going to happen tomorrow, he should probably be awake for it. He closed his eyes, wrapping his finger around the bow so that no one could steal the package without waking him. He was already asleep when the bus rolled out onto the street, the sun slipping below the earth and plunging everything into darkness.

THIS TIME HE DREAMT of his own father and mother and the night he'd received the news of their death, and there was a tear running down his cheek when he awoke. He missed his mom and dad, at least what he could remember of them. Their memory made him miss Joseph that much more, his goofy smile, the fierceness of his embrace, and the love and trust burning in his eyes.

The interior lights of the bus were turned low, and Jack saw that most people were either sleeping or reading. He turned his attention out the window and could make out city lights in the distance. He was stepping off the bus and stretching fifteen minutes later.

He stood before the map that was hanging on the terminal wall. It offered a more detailed street plan than the one folded up in his pocket, and he realized that a rental car would be the right choice if not for it requiring a credit card. If "they" were still looking for him, then tipping them off to his being in Connecticut might give them an idea of what he was up to. And "they" would probably want to prevent him from opening that can of worms. So it would be a long walk down Asylum Ave.

Asylum Avenue, he mused. What were the chances of that? *The House of Thunder*—a Soviet plot involving a false reality—came suggesting unpleasant theories again. Bears, books, conspirators, and now street names. Was his subconscious pulling familiar material from his life and twisting it with clues meant to wake him up from such a coma? Is that how he'd managed to run into a member of the Don't Tread On Me family in some backwoods restaurant?

He left the terminal, found Asylum Avenue, and began walking down the sidewalk. Ten miles. He should make it just in time for brunch. He wondered if he should stop and pick up some coffee and donuts. *Surprise, honey! It's me! I brought coffee!*

The sun climbed a partly cloudy sky, and the cool morning breeze felt good on his face. But even though Jack escaped the heart of the city without a run-in with government assassins, he found that his heart was beating faster and faster.

26

ASYLUM AVENUE CONNECTED WITH Albany Turnpike, and Albany Turnpike led to the street of the estate. Climax Road it was called, and that eerily fitting name haunted Jack all through the woods that ran along its side, pestering him until he reached a white concrete driveway that came snaking across his path. He turned and followed it while making sure to stay within the shadow of the woods. He was sure there were surveillance cameras around the property.

As the giant house appeared through the tree line like pieces of a jigsaw puzzle, Jack became conscious of his sweat-stained shirt and the awful odor that was clinging to it. It wasn't exactly part of his ideal reunion scenario. Maybe he should take it off, go in all bare-chested like some Hollywood action hero. *You're a salesman*, he reminded himself.

He decided to keep the shirt on. He dropped to a knee and unwrapped the package, freeing the pistol. He chambered a round and tucked it into the back of his pants, then got to his feet and made his way to the edge of the trees. There, he stood gazing at the property. At the manicured lawn sweeping away from him. At the driveway ending in a circle at the front of the house. At the fountain flowing from the circle's center. At the large Roman columns and armies of bright flowers and sculpted bushes circling the three-story residence. Maybe this was what Stacey left him for. If he waited long enough, would he see a silver Aston Martin DB5 pull out from around the back of the estate, some handsome playboy with one hand on the steering wheel, the other around his wife?

The front door swung open.

A man stepped out between the colonnades. Jack dropped back to his knees. The man was wearing a polo shirt tucked into khaki shorts, sandals on his feet. Even from his position, Jack could see the polo being stretched across the Russian's large chest.

Joining him was an attractive blonde. She stepped out of the house and took his hand.

Stacey.

Jack's heart stopped at the sight of her. There she was, right in front of him. And before he realized it, he was actually stepping out from behind the cover of the trees, her presence attracting him like a moth to flame. His heart ached for her, and he needed to touch her, to hold her. He needed to cry and to kiss her. *There she is.* But instead of her running toward him with arms open wide, she was descending the steps hand-in-hand with some tall Russian and heading up the driveway.

The sharp sting of betrayed love tightened his chest. He dropped back into shadow and waited for them to pass because inside him was also a curiosity that needed to know the whys and hows. And he wouldn't leave this place until he knew them all.

Once Stacey (*Anna!*) and Vadim—at least he assumed it was Vadim—were out of sight, heading toward the road, Jack sprinted across the lawn, past the fountain, and up the stairs to the door. It was unlocked. That made him pause for a second. It didn't seem like a double-agent kind of thing to do. Unless he had security guards patrolling the estate... He pulled the pistol out and pushed open the door.

The inside seemed even bigger than the outside, and Jack wondered how Vadim had managed to end up in such a place. Either his cover job was a really good one, or the CIA was sparing no expense in purchasing his loyalty. He swore and kept still, listening for signs of dogs or guards. The house was quiet.

And though he'd come in without a plan, he was now trying to figure out the best way of shooting Vadim when he returned. Should he jump out behind him as soon as he stepped in, tapping him in the back of the head? Should he open the door for them and just put one between his eyes? Either way, the spy had to die so that he could get the whole story from Stacey—the true story. But no, not necessarily... With Vadim dead, if Stacey had run off with the SVR agent, then at that point she would just tell him whatever he wanted to hear. Which might or might not be the truth. He abandoned his plot to kill Vadim and instead began searching for signs of Joseph.

Ignoring the wooden steps that circled up to the next floor, he left the foyer and its obnoxious chandelier behind. He passed closed doors on either side of him and found himself in a cigar room. He aimed the pistol back and forth, the dark-hued shades that covered the windows casting the room in a crimson glow. Bookshelves decorated the walls, a globe sat on a cherry-red desk, and small sculptures replicating famous art he didn't recognize stood as sentries in the corners. Spinning around, Jack could see a sunlit expanse at the other end of a long hallway and guessed it to be the kitchen. He went that way, gun held out in front of him.

The kitchen was almost the size of his house. But then he remembered that he didn't have a house anymore. There was a large table placed in an alcove that was surrounded on three sides by floor-to-ceiling windows, the rest of the gourmet kitchen as big as a tennis court.

A noise came from somewhere else in the house.

He quickly ducked out of the kitchen and into another room. Maybe the living room, or at least one of them. It was remarkable, whatever it was. Huge cathedral-like windows were fanned out across the far wall, offering a more-than-adequate view of the Connecticut woods. A glass coffee table sat in the center of the room, a stone fireplace watching over it.

More books were climbing the walls, and exotic plants were arranged to keep them company. Couches, chairs, and footstools... He pictured his wife and Vadim spending their nights here.

"Well, well, well... Look what the tide washed ashore."

The voice was all too familiar, and Jack didn't need to turn around in order to identify it. But of course, he did turn around and leveled the pistol right at her face.

"Hello, Viktoriya," he said. "Or is it *Natasha*?"

She was sitting in a large white chair that dwarfed her frame. She was wearing white herself, so it was no wonder that his cursory sweep of the room had missed her. She had a short glass in her hand; her legs were crossed. She smiled and an unfamiliar warmth seemed to fill her gray eyes.

"Sit down, Jack," she ordered calmly.

He stole a look out the huge windows, expecting to see his wife and her Russian husband approaching with guns drawn, good ol' Viki having alerted them to his presence.

But she shook her head. "They'll be gone for a little while yet. They walk to a coffee shop that's about two miles away.

Frankly, I think it's reckless." She shrugged as if to say, but who am I? Which was a position Jack had never known her to take on anything.

He sat down on the couch across from her. Rested the 9 mm on his lap where she could see it. "What the hell is going on, Viktoriya? Where's Joseph?" She seemed to regard him with a strange apathy, and he thought she might be stalling.

She took a sip of the caramel-colored liquid and then turned her gaze out the window, staring off beyond the trees and into her own thoughts. "I'm glad you're here." It was almost a whisper.

"And why would that be?"

She smiled, the lines in her face stretching taut. "I always liked you, Jack."

"You never liked me."

She didn't rebut him, only cast her eyes to the floor. "How did you..."

"Survive being tossed overboard?"

She nodded.

Jack wasn't sure what was going on, but the Russian countess had dissolved into a frail, tired, old woman. "I guess someone saw my naked body careening through the moonlight. The ship turned around and came back for me." Her eyes swept back to him, and again, he saw something that he'd never seen there before.

"I'm sorry you had to go through that. I know it must have been torture believing that she was dead."

"Yeah, it's been a pretty crappy week. You wanna tell me why you put us on that ship to begin with?"

She took another sip. Her eyes returned to the unseen and the gravity of whatever it contained. She raised her index finger as though she was remembering something she didn't want to later forget. "Joseph is upstairs." She set the liquid in the glass swirling. "He's been sleeping in lately. It's been tough on him. He really misses you."

The news set water pooling in his eyes and a spreading warmth through his chest. He was about to get to his feet, but she told him to stay.

"He is fine, and I have a story to tell."

Jack stared at her, trying to resist storming up the stairs and getting Joseph out of here. He glanced out the window and to the driveway again, just making sure Vadim wasn't about to launch a shoulder-mounted rocket through the window at him. "Okay."

Viktoriya settled back in the chair and began, "My husband, Stacey's father, was KGB."

"I know."

And she squinted at him, as if she was just now asking herself how he'd found them.

"I got the FBI involved."

"The FBI?" She seemed surprised.

"Yeah, but the CIA railroaded them."

"Ah." She nodded as if it made perfect sense. "Well, I'm sure they didn't find out everything." She licked her thin lips. "My husband's name was Dmitri Aleksandrov. Stacey, or *Anna*..."

He nodded, indicating that he'd discovered that as well, and she continued.

"We had her in 1974, and I eventually brought her to New York. A couple of years before Dmitri died."

"The FBI told me all that."

"Did they tell you that I was a plant?"

No, they hadn't told him that. He leaned forward. "What?"

"I was an agent for the KGB myself."

That was a shot to his blindside, and it rendered him paralyzed for a second.

"Stacey doesn't know," she continued.

"*Didn't* know."

"Doesn't."

The Connecticut geography was beginning to shift below his feet.

"Vadim Sidorov came over in the mid '90s as an active agent. Stacey didn't know it. *I* didn't know it. Though I suppose I should have suspected it. All the signs were there." She looked him in the eye, as if knowing the next part of her story would cause a reaction. "They met in New York and got married in '99."

No reaction.

"You knew this?" she asked.

"Yeah. I found—" and he stopped himself. "Just keep talking."

"He was okay," she said. "At least he was Russian."

Ah...

But she waved the thought away once she saw it cross his face. "The CIA found him in 2005 and turned the bastard." She paused and took another sip. "That's when Stacey learned who he really was, that he was a spy. And in order to protect her, he sent her away with me. If the SVR learned that he'd been turned...well, he didn't want to have to worry about Anna. We moved to Philadelphia the same year."

Jack couldn't believe that she was talking about his wife. *His own wife!* Might as well be talking about some random woman picked out of a phone book! He didn't even know her.

"By that time, she didn't want anything to do with him anymore. Her love had been young and blind, and she wasn't able to see through the mask he wore. Not until later. Not until she witnessed firsthand the ruthlessness he'd kept hidden from her." Her slender shoulders lifted in a shrug. "And she wanted to settle down and start a family. She never signed up to be the wife of a double agent, always having to look over her shoulder. So when he sent her away, she decided to leave him for good."

He had a fingerhold on a rung. The ladder itself was uncertain, but at least he wasn't free-falling anymore.

"Then she met you."

He leaned forward more, hanging on every accented syllable that fluttered from her KGB lips.

"She loved you. *Loves* you." Her eyes seemed to be pinned to the floor by a heavy sense of guilt. "In 2007, they found out that Vadim was working for the Central Intelligence Agency, and they activated me."

"The SVR?"

She nodded. "Officially, the KGB was disbanded in 1991. But in reality, the SVR just took over where it left off. Anyway, my mission was to eliminate Vadim. And I can only assume they chose me because of our unique relationship." She shook her head ever so slightly. She pursed her lips. "What are the odds that my daughter ends up marrying an agent here? One of the reasons we took the mission was because we saw it as a way to give our daughter a way out. And she unknowingly married right back into it all." She took a moment to collect herself, staring into her drink. "Anna was scheduled to go on a business trip a few days later, so I contacted Vadim. I told him that she missed him and wanted to see him, that it would be a wonderful surprise if he just showed up. And I gave him the hotel she was to be staying at."

"Did he know she was married to me?" He tried to recall Stacey going away on a business trip in 2007 but wasn't coming up with anything.

"No. If he knew that, then he might have killed her. Which is why when Vadim showed up, Anna had no choice but to play along. Knowing nothing about my mission, she played the role of dutiful wife."

"Meaning?"

"She shared her bed with him."

Jack's heart filled with something explosive, and the pressure in his chest mounted. The last five years...

"She had to, Jack. They were still married. If he knew about you..."

"Why? Why did you set them up?"

"I booked a room in the same hotel, and I waited for an opportunity to either poison him or shoot him with a silenced pistol. But I never got a chance. He was careful."

Jack raised a shaking hand to his mouth. *I haven't gotten this drunk since Joseph was conceived...* "Was she drinking a lot?"

"It was the only way she could get through it. She hated every second she was with him, and she felt like she was cheating on you. She drank more than I've ever seen her drink." She spoke the words as if they would relieve him in some way, and maybe they would have. If not for what they implied.

Silence settled between them.

"Is Joseph my son?"

His mother-in-law pressed her lips together as her eyes lit up with revelation. "Oh my god..." She quickly began shaking her head. "No. I mean, I don't know. I guess it was about the same time that she must have conceived, but...I don't know. She never told me about those two days. She has carried that shame all by herself. As have I."

"Holy—" Jack leaned back, speechless. He locked his fingers behind his head and tried to keep it from spinning off. His fingerhold on the ladder slipped, and he was falling into hell again. Joseph... All the traits he loved so much in him, all the idiosyncrasies, the gentle mannerisms, all the things that made him the apple of his eye...were from *Vadim*? He wanted to puke. He wanted to pick up the glass coffee table and throw it through the huge windows.

Tears of frustration began spilling from the corners of his eyes. His best buddy in the whole world, his little four-year-old boy, was a fraud. An impostor. A lie. His real father a Russian spy! His eyes clawed their way back up to hers. "Does she know I'm alive?"

"No."

He smirked beneath the teardrops. "She looked pretty content just then, walking hand-in-hand with her other husband like some little—"

"She doesn't have a choice."

"What do you mean? He'll kill her?"

"Joseph."

He tried to navigate his brain around the swells of indignation. "Is he that dangerous?"

"He was always a little unstable. Like I said, she's afraid of him. Afraid of the CIA and afraid of the SVR. She's trapped,

Jack. And all she can do is pretend that everything is okay now that she has been reunited with her husband."

"What would he do if he found out about me?"

"Oh, he knows about you now. That was unavoidable. That's why you were thrown off the ship. She had to make him believe that she never loved you, that she only married you for your last name and the new identity that came with it. He believes that she was using you. Again, for Joseph's sake, as well as her own well-being, she doesn't have a choice in this."

"Why now?"

Viktoriya leaned forward, finished the remains of whatever was in her glass, and stood. She made her way to the fireplace, taking her time getting there and leaning heavily against it once she did. Her back was to him. "Once I failed to kill him, the SVR decided on another strategy, one they hoped would have the CIA chasing its own tail."

He shifted on the couch so that he could see her. "Disinformation."

"Recently, the CIA or some other intelligence department within the US government wanted him to help them carry out some kind of mission. He was happy to help them on one condition. He wanted Anna back. They were happy to oblige."

Jack stood on shaky legs. "It was the CIA that threw me overboard?"

"CIA, NSA...I don't know. The SVR suspected that Vadim was going to be the patsy for a false-flag operation cooked up by some maniacs in the Pentagon." She paused and turned to face him. As she turned, she pulled a silenced pistol from out of the white bathrobe.

Jack quickly raised his pistol.

Viktoriya didn't seem to notice. "They activated me again. This time they said failure would not be an advisable option. When an intelligence agency says something like that, Jack, there is no missing the threat."

He lowered the Smith & Wesson a bit. "Why did you send us on the cruise?"

"They came to me one day...the CIA or whoever. They had this whole plan of how they were going to get Anna back to Vadim while at the same time erasing her past. It was a rather creative plan if not unnecessarily complicated. They switched her normal mammogram with one that revealed breast cancer, and then they gave me the money and story needed to get you out into the middle of the ocean. Where you could be made to disappear. The cruise line wouldn't investigate, and all other jurisdiction was up in the air. They could do whatever they wanted, and no one would even bat an eye. I was to take Joseph and rendezvous with Anna and Vadim here."

She set the empty glass down on the fireplace and clutched the mantel for support. "I thought all of this was behind me," she whispered. "I had moved on. I never thought they would contact me again..." She looked up at him, and there were actual tears in her eyes. "They made threats against Anna and Joseph if I didn't cooperate." A drop fell. "I am so sorry, Jack."

This really is a spy story. "Who was the one using the computer to look up plane tickets and driving directions—"

"Red herrings. Just in case."

"They burnt down the house."

"What?"

"And killed Ivan and Donny."

"Dear God..." she muttered. "I..." She couldn't seem to get anything out, and her mind tripped over the reach of this thing she'd been coerced to start.

"Did Stacey write the suicide note?"

She refocused. "The agents, if not Russian, were at least fluent in Russian, and she believed that they worked for

Vadim, that they were bringing her back to him. At that point, her only concern was protecting Joseph."

There were so many questions Jack wanted to ask, but his head was spinning too crazily to get a handle on any one thought. Instead, he focused on the gun in her hand. "What are you gonna do?"

"If some crackpot in the US government," she said stoically, "is planning a false-flag attack in order to justify some kind of action against Russia, then I will do my part to prevent it."

"If that's the case, I think they might have bagged the operation after the FBI started nosing around."

Viktoriya shook her head. "It's not a chance Russia is willing to take." She smiled. "It is ironic that you showed up today, Jack. Why don't you go see Joseph."

He hesitated, trying to get a feel for what her intentions were. Then movement from outside caught his attention. They were coming back.

"Go be with Joseph," Viktoriya said. "And if something should happen to me... please be sure to always let him know how much I loved him."

"Viktoriya..."

"Just go, Jack."

He didn't argue. He slipped the pistol back into his pants and left the room. He found the stairs and took them two at a time. They led him to a room packed with toys and children's books, posters of Joseph's favorite Disney characters decorating the walls, and stepped into it. He closed the door behind him. When he turned around, he found the bed. And there he was, curled up with a thumb in his mouth, and his eyes closed.

He went and sat on the edge of the bed, tears running down his face, and ran a gentle hand over Joseph's head. He leaned down and kissed him. A tear fell from the tip of his nose and splashed against Joseph's cheek. *Thank you, God.* His boy was okay.

But a dark voice within challenged him on that. *Your boy?* it asked.

But he knew now that none of that mattered. He had held Joseph in his arms when he was all bloody and covered in crap, squirming like an alien still attached to the mother ship. A spiritual bond that no words could define had formed between them in that moment, and it was a bond that Jack wasn't about to walk away from. Joseph was his son and would forever remain his son. "I love you, buddy," he whispered.

There was a window in the room that overlooked the driveway, and Jack got up and moved to it. He could see Stacey and Vadim just twenty yards away, approaching the circle with coffee cups in hand. Stacey was wearing a thin sundress that the breeze was pulling tight against her body, accentuating her female features. Her hair was sunlit and waved behind her like a comet's tail of gold. Jack fought hard to breathe, unable to take his eyes off her. She still held the keys to his heart, and he knew right then that he wasn't going to leave this place without her.

As the two Russians walked past the fountain, Jack finally managed to pry his eyes off her and let them fall over the Soviet imposter. Who at the same time looked up at him.

Jack ducked below the frame. Had he been seen?

"Daddy?"

Joseph was sitting up in bed, staring at him through a mask of corked emotion. Jack ran to the bed and swept the boy into his arms. "I'm here, buddy," he whispered. Joseph buried his head against his neck, and Jack could feel the tears running down his shirt, shattering his heart. He squeezed him tighter. "I'm here. Everything's okay."

"I missed you, Daddy," Joseph cried.

Jack pulled out of the embrace and looked into the boy's eyes. "I love you so much."

"I love you, too."

"Are you okay?"

He nodded and lunged forward, wrapping his tiny arms around his daddy's neck again.

After laying an affectionate kiss on his cheek, Jack said, "I need you to do me a favor, okay?" He felt Joseph's head move up and down. "I need you to climb back in bed and stay there for a few minutes, okay? I need to go downstairs and check on Mommy." He set him back down on the bed. "Okay?"

Joseph looked up into his eyes, tears still streaming down his face. "I don't want to pretend that man is you anymore, Daddy."

Jack swallowed back the wave of emotion and forced a smile. "You don't have to, buddy. I'm here now, and we're going home in a little bit."

"We're gonna miss the Yankees game, aren't we?"

"We'll go to another one, I promise. Now stay here until I come back for you, okay?"

"Okay, Daddy."

Jack left the room. He pulled the pistol out of his pants and crept to the stairs. As he got closer, he could make out Stacey's voice echoing up to him from somewhere below. She was speaking Russian, so he didn't know what she was saying, but he could tell that she was agitated about something. He started down the stairs.

Two more voices—a man's and another woman's. They were shouting at each other, and though Jack couldn't make sense of it, he knew that things were escalating fast.

Something crashed. Glass shattered. Stacey screamed.

Jack flew down the remaining stairs in pursuit of the commotion. He found himself in a room that led to the kitchen, where he could tell the fighting was coming from. He ran to the end of the hallway but stopped short of entering the room. The huge island counter was directly in front of him, the voices coming from around the corner to his right. And then Viktoriya came flying into his line of sight. She crashed into the island, her feet flying up over her head. She landed hard on the floor, her silenced pistol spinning across the tile. She moaned as she struggled to move. Red freckles dotted her white robe, and it was torn where it had gotten caught on one of the island's burners.

Jack could still hear Stacey and Vadim shouting at each other. And then the unmistakable sound of a face being slapped put an abrupt end to the argument.

The floodgates of rage he'd been trying to keep closed over the past few days suddenly burst open wide, his wife being slapped the dynamite blowing them to pieces and allowing the surging tide to carry him into the kitchen. As he walked through the doorway, rounding the corner, he saw Stacey bent forward over the countertop, Vadim pressed up against her from behind and pulling her hair. Whatever he was saying, she obviously didn't like, but she was pinned and powerless to do anything about it. Vadim had one hand in her hair and the other pressing tight against his side, blood seeping between his fingers and splashing onto the floor at their feet. Viktoriya had shot him.

Jack screamed with the fury of a hurricane. "Hey!" He raised the gun.

The Russian turned his head toward him but didn't release or move away from

Stacey. "You must be Jack." His accent was barely recognizable.

"Take your hands off her, or I'll kill you." He was so angry that his hands were shaking, and he wondered if he was more likely to put a bullet in the sink than in Vadim's eye.

Stacey tried to turn her head his way, to see him, but Vadim slammed her head down onto the counter. She cried out.

Jack pulled the trigger. The loud blast turned everyone quiet, drywall dust falling out of the ceiling and settling in Vadim's hair.

Vadim started to laugh. "You can't do it, can you? Shoot me?"

Jack stepped forward. "I'm here, Stacey. Everything's going to be okay."

"Jack…how did…" She reached for some degree of understanding, but under the present circumstances, her head being pressed onto the marble countertop, she couldn't seem to get a firm grip on anything.

"Shut up, whore!" Vadim yanked her head back by her hair. Then thrust her face into the wooden cabinets hanging over the counter.

Jack had been aiming for Vadim's head the first time, but he'd pulled instead of squeezed the trigger and the barrel jumped. He wouldn't make that mistake again. He began squeezing...

Vadim grabbed Stacey, flung her in front of him like a shield. His free hand clasped her neck like a vise.

Jack lowered the gun a little.

"You want this little tramp?" Vadim asked, smirking as he reached his bloody hand around and groped her left breast.

She struggled against him, but even with a bullet in him, he was too strong for her.

His hand fell away from her chest, leaving a red handprint, and reached down between her legs. He smiled as she squirmed. "What was she like for you, Jack?"

Jack stepped closer, rage bringing the pistol back up. But it was a ridiculous gesture. He was just as likely to kill Stacey as he was Vadim. And Vadim knew it. Which was why he was laughing more.

He lifted the back of her dress up to her shoulder blades. "Want to watch?"

Jack tried skirting right for a clearer shot, but they were in the corner of the kitchen, walls on either side protecting the double agent. But he had to do something. He couldn't just stand there and watch...

Vadim tore her underwear off, and she screamed as the fabric snapped against her hips.

"Listen," she started to say. "Vadim, I'll do whatever you want, baby. I love you. I don't care about him! You want me to prove it?" She turned around so that she was facing him. "Darling..." and she started speaking in Russian again.

Jack didn't know what she was saying, but it seemed to be making some kind of impression on Vadim. He looked at Jack and sneered again. Then he nodded, and Stacey hopped up, wrapping her legs around him. She kissed him hard on the mouth while struggling to unbuckle his belt.

Jack took a step back. He knew that if he were to charge, the Russian bear would no doubt have him disarmed in less than a second. Then he'd shoot him with his own gun.

Vadim was just staring at him, daring him to try something.

There was a *thhooot! thhooot!* and a wet smack as something struck Vadim's side. He grunted and bent forward, sending Stacey falling off him. She landed on her back with a gasp as the air left her lungs.

Looking up, Vadim swept his burning eyes over to Viktoriya, who was lying on her stomach beside the island, both arms outstretched and holding her smoking pistol. She got off another shot, but it missed his head, crashing into the cabinets instead. He spun, reached onto the counter and pulled a steak knife from a wooden block resting nearby. He threw it at the same time she got off her next shot.

Viktoriya's bullet found his shoulder, but his knife found her right eye. She reached for her face, her fingers dancing over the blade for a moment, but she fell still before she could get a grasp on it.

Stacey let loose a gut-wrenching wail and stumbled to her feet. She ran to her mother's side.

Vadim reached for another knife.

And all Jack could do was stand there and watch, the pistol aimed but not shooting, everything happening too fast. Vadim selected another long knife from the block and turned.

Come on! Shoot him!

The Russian took a step toward him, blood seeping from three separate holes, his shorts half undone.

But then Jack realized he couldn't shoot him. If his bullet, from his registered gun, killed this CIA black operative, then... Well, he wasn't sure what the ramifications would be, but he was relatively certain they wouldn't be good. He'd paid careful attention to cover his tracks up to this point, and he had no intention of signing his name on this guy's corpse now.

He turned and ran from the kitchen.

But Vadim didn't follow. Instead, he went stumbling through another room.

Was he going for the front door? Was he going to try to make a run for it through the woods?

Jack put it together too late.

No.

He sprinted through the house, searching for the foyer and the staircase, but a few wrong turns through more rooms had him completely spun around. By the time he found the stairs, Vadim was at the top of them, a trail of blood behind him.

Jack took the stairs as fast as he could and heard the door to Joseph's room slam shut just as he reached the hallway.

No!

He ran to the door and reached out for the doorknob. When his fingers fell on it, a train slammed against him, plowing him in the side and putting him halfway through the wall and into the adjoining room. The gun fell from his hand, and all he could see were shining stars. Everything spun out of control. It took him a few seconds to realize he was being struck in the face, that Vadim was on him and throwing Russian fist after Russian fist into his face. He could taste the blood trickling down the back of his throat, and he tried raising his hands to slow the attack. It was useless, and Vadim's demonic face began fading to black.

The bear had won.

WHEN JACK OPENED HIS eyes, the first thing he saw was the door to Joseph's room standing open. Summoning the willpower to move, he struggled to his knees and crawled to the threshold. The earthquake in his head made the short journey almost unbearable. His eyes were swollen shut, and he could taste the metallic flavor of blood as it poured from his face, staining the carpet below him. Once his hand crossed the border that separated Joseph's room from the hallway, Vadim's voice sounded out, startling him.

"I didn't kill you because I wanted you to see this first."

Jack lifted his head and found the man standing in the middle of the room. He was standing behind Joseph, one arm wrapped around his frail waist, the other pressing the knife against his throat.

Vadim's eyes flickered with hatred. "He's yours, isn't he?"

"No," Jack answered. He reached out a hand, pleading. "He's *your* son."

Joseph was crying, and a puddle spread around one of his bare feet.

Vadim flashed a wicked smile. "Lies."

"No!" Jack stammered through Stacey's two days with him in 2007. "He's yours. Don't do this! He's *your* son!" He was sobbing, completely helpless to stop what he knew was coming.

Vadim grabbed a tuft of the boy's hair and yanked his head to the side so that he could get a better look at him. Seemingly unconvinced, he said, "Well, then you won't really mind, will you?" He ran the knife across Joseph's throat, and a thin red line chased after it.

Even as Jack's scream filled the house, a door on the other side of the room burst open. Stacey stepped in, coming up behind Vadim and firing Viki's silenced pistol into the back of his head.

Joseph dropped onto his side—his young, innocent eyes full of shock and incomprehension—as Vadim's head blew apart. Bone sprayed like shrapnel throughout the room. Blood and pink tissue splattered stuffed animals and Disney posters. The Russian collapsed to the floor, the soup bowl that was his head staring up at the ceiling.

Stacey dropped the gun and collapsed beside Joseph. She pulled her dress up and over her head.

Jack crawled to them, tears blinding his eyes, reaching for Joseph's hands. Finding one, he squeezed. Joseph's eyes found his, and they seemed to beg for some kind of understanding, for help. Stacey was wrapping her dress around his neck and pulling it tight. The thin fabric turned red instantly.

The knife gliding across Joseph's neck replayed in Jack's mind, and he thought it was a miracle his head hadn't come off. Or maybe Vadim had held up at the last possible moment, second-guessing himself.

"Call an ambulance!" Stacey was screaming.

The total desperation in her voice snapped Jack out of his stupor. He rushed crazily to his feet and clambered out of the room, blood streaking the walls wherever he touched them for support. "Where is it?" he cried back over his shoulder, a red mist spraying from his mouth as he shouted.

"Kitchen!"

He ran down half the stairs and vaulted himself over the banister, landing sprawled out on the carpet below. He scrambled back to his feet, the pain in his body completely lost to the fear of losing his son. *No*, he told himself. Not after everything he'd been through. Not like this! He found the phone on the wall in the kitchen and dialed 911 so fast that he was afraid he might have hit one of the numbers too many times. But an operator answered, and Jack blurted out the address and what had happened. Without waiting to hear a response, he dropped the phone and rushed back to his son, ignoring his mother-in-law sprawled out on the floor in a puddle of blood, the knife like some horror-movie prop still sticking out of her face.

When he entered the room, panting and struggling for breath, Stacey was sitting on the floor with Joseph's head in her lap. She was staring down at him, humming and running her fingers through his hair. Joseph's eyes were closed.

Jack dropped to his knees beside them, and Stacey moved her eyes to his. Tears were spilling down her cheeks, but she didn't stop humming. Jack grabbed Joseph's hand and held it tight. He kissed it and brought it against his cheek. "Hang in there, buddy. The ambulance is on its way. Just hold on, okay? Everything's gonna be all right." But that was what he'd said before, wasn't it?

Five minutes later, when the sound of sirens came storming the estate, Joseph was still alive. Every drop of blood that fell, however, was a drop closer to the unthinkable. Stacey leaned down and kissed his forehead. "Hold on, baby...hold on." Tears landed on his eyelids.

When banging sounded on the door downstairs, Jack stood, Joseph's hand sliding out of his own, and ran to open it.

Just before opening the door, he had an involuntary thought streak through his brain, one that involved making a run for it. But that was no longer possible with Joseph bleeding out on the floor. It was time to face the music—no matter what song it might be. Maybe, depending on how Joseph was making out, he'd think of something at the hospital, a story that might discourage further attention from the CIA. But then, wouldn't they be listening to Vadim's house calls and already know about the 911 call?

It didn't matter. With her son moments away from death, shooting her first husband, seeing her mother killed, and witnessing her second husband come back from the dead all within a five-minute span of time, Jack was sure that Stacey was far from being up to playing make-believe.

He opened the door, pointed up the stairs, and watched the men race to save his son's life. He only wanted Joseph to live.

Please, God...

27

THEY WERE AT A hospital in Hartford. Police kept stopping by, trying to figure out what had happened, asking them questions. But neither of them were capable of answering anything. Not until the doctor came out and gave them the news that Joseph was going to be okay. Only then did they both start the slow journey back to the world around them. Stitches and a couple of days in the hospital, the doctor had reported. Apparently, he said, the man who did this either hesitated at the last second or never intended to kill their son.

Jack took her hand in his, and a small smile broke through the weight of all she'd endured. "I guess I have some explaining to do," she said.

"When you're ready. You've been through a lot." When she didn't say anything, he said, "I'm sorry about your mother."

A tear rolled off her chin, but she didn't respond to the statement. Instead, she grabbed the back of his neck with her free hand and looked into his eyes with all the surprise of his being there. "You're *alive*."

"Turns out, I'm a pretty decent swimmer. Took me a few days and a generous jellyfish, but I made it."

Her eyes broke away from his and dropped to her feet. "I guess you know that I was married before."

"Vadim."

"I'm so sorry."

"Shhhh... We don't have to talk about this now." He wrapped his arms around her and pulled her close, unable to believe that he was actually holding her again. Tears accompanied his words when he spoke them. "I thought they threw you over, too. I spent three days in the Bahamas smashed out of my mind." He felt her squeeze him tighter.

"I need to tell you now—" she sighed "—before the FBI gets here. You deserve to know. God, after all these years, you deserve to know."

He looked around the waiting room and was satisfied that no one was listening. “Okay.”

Not letting go of him, she spoke softly into his ear. “I was married to Vadim before I met you. It was a mistake. I was young, and I found out too late who he really was.”

“SVR.”

She seemed surprised that he knew this. “How—”

“Finish your story, and then I’ll tell you mine.”

She leaned back and settled into her own seat, brushed a strand of hair away from her eyes. “It was more than that, though. He had a dark side to him.”

Really? he almost asked, but he bit his tongue. The way Viktoriya had died was nothing to joke about. Neither was his son’s throat being slashed.

“I was scared,” she continued. “When the CIA turned him...” She stopped herself when Jack didn’t even flinch at that. “How much of this do you know?”

“Keep going. I’ll stop you when I hear something that bears repeating.”

“Okay,” she said, suspicious. “When the CIA made him a double agent, I knew it might be my only chance to get away, so I convinced him that I should lie low somewhere, made him think I was afraid of the SVR finding out he'd been compromised. I acted paranoid enough to sow some fear in his own mind, and he finally agreed that I should disappear for a while. So I took my mother to Philadelphia. And then I met you."

Jack wished he could shake Donny's hand and tell him with all the pride of a happy husband that he'd been right in his counsel to trust her. Of all the possible theories trying to explain Stacey's involvement in all this nonsense, the truth had turned out to be as good as it could've been.

Donny... That storm was still brewing out over the horizon.

"I didn't tell you because...it didn't seem fair. To make you worry. And the way you are, *Jerry*, you would've never gotten past it. You'd be looking over your shoulder forever." She fell silent for a moment. "I should've told you before we got married. Given you a choice...but I was afraid I'd lose you..."

Jack ran his hands through her hair, brushing tears off her face with his thumb. He stared at her for a whole minute, regretting every vengeful thought he'd had against her over the last few days. *Love believes all things, hopes all things...* Amen.

But there was still that one thing that needed knowing. As much as he didn't want to ask, he understood that the road to full recovery had to start now, whatever the answer was.

"Stacey," he began.

She looked up into his eyes.

"I know about what happened with Vadim in 2007."

New tears dropped from her eyes, and shame forced her to divert her gaze once more.

"Is Joseph my son?" The words came half choked by the long cave they seemed to travel from.

"It was only one time, Jack. I was away for work, and he just showed up at the hotel." She took her time, still not looking at him. "My mother thought we needed to 'catch up.' She took the liberty of telling him where I was. I always thought that she secretly wanted me to leave you and go back to Vadim."

Jack held his tongue. Should he tell her the truth?

She began sobbing, and though Jack wanted to reassure her by taking her hand, he couldn't bring himself to do it. Not yet.

"He didn't know about you," she cried. "And I couldn't tell him. It was all I could do to get the rings off in time. If he knew about you, he'd kill you. Or me. So I pretended that I was glad to see him and kept asking when he thought it would be safe for me to come back to him, that I couldn't stand being without him. It made me sick to say, and I could've killed my mother. I had to..." Her hands swiped the tears away as they descended, but some slipped through and dropped to the floor at their feet.

"Joseph..." It was the only word Jack could get out.

She shook her head. "It was right around the time I got pregnant, and..." She swore. "I wasn't sure. I had a test taken after he was born. I had to know. I mean, I didn't want to know, just in case, but..." She looked up and offered a pathetic attempt at a smile. "He's your son, Jack." And then she let out a noise that was one part laughter and one part crying.

He released the breath he was holding, and the weight of the world flew off him so fast that he felt like a feather caught up in a twister. He smiled and made his own contribution to the puddle of tears between them. "I would've loved him like he was my own, anyway," he said, embracing her again.

"I know," she whispered. "I know."

"When we were on the boat, you said that you were drunk when Joseph was conceived."

"I did?" She shook her head. "I must've been confused. I *was* drunk with him. It was the only way I could do it. But for Joseph's sake, I had to make myself believe that..." She looked desperately into his eyes, begging him to believe her. "Please, I was confused. You're his father. I'll show you the test results."

"What about the books and letters you kept hidden in your closet?"

"You found them?"

"Well, the guy who came to burn down the house found them."

"They burned down our house?" she shouted.

Some of the cops turned their heads. "Later. Why keep them?"

"What do you mean later? Did they burn down our house?"

He looked around. "Shhh. Yeah. What about the letters?"

It took her a moment to get her mind off the house. "I had to keep them in case he ever showed up. I needed to be able to convince him that I was waiting for him.

At least until I could figure something else out."

"And what were the books?"

"Just stupid novels we liked. Before I knew who he really was, we kind of had this hobby..."

"Finding novels with Soviet plots?"

She nodded. "It was stupid." Then she looked at him, her eyes warming again. "I can't believe you're actually here. I thought you drowned. I tried to stop them, but they dragged me out of the room. I was screaming for you to wake up."

"What about the suicide note?"

"They made me. Vadim's men. After they threw you overboard, they told me who they were, that they were taking me back to Vadim. He knew about you and Joseph, and he wasn't too happy. They said they'd kill Joseph if I didn't go along with them."

The skin across Jack's brow furrowed.

"What?"

"Nothing." Did she not know about the CIA's involvement in all this? He wondered if Johnson and Viktoriya could have been wrong. But there was no way Vadim had the resources to pull this off on his own. Which meant that Stacey didn't know what the CIA was setting

Vadim up for. He guessed no one would ever know. "You convinced him that Joseph was his?"

"Yeah, but I don't think he ever really believed it. He wanted to, though. I told him I didn't love you, that I was just using you. I said I was so scared the SVR was going to find me that I needed to disappear, take on a new identity while I waited for him to figure something out. Not sure he really believed that, either."

She fell silent, and Jack could almost see the images flashing through her mind. Images of her first husband's head exploding as she put a few bullets into the back of it. Images of her mother with a steak knife sticking out of her eye. Images of Joseph bleeding all over the place.

"Do you know that you don't really have cancer?"

She didn't say anything, but Jack could tell she stopped breathing.

"It was part of the plot to get us on the cruise."

"They doctored the mammogram?"

"It was someone else's." He'd tell her about Timonen later. "You're healthy. No cancer."

A small smile tugged at the corner of her lips as she let it sink in.

Another detective walked in, and Jack didn't want to talk to him. He knew he wouldn't be able to hold them off much longer, but he only needed a few more minutes." You wanna get some coffee?" There were still a couple of things they had to go over, like her father and her mother.

"Yeah." She took his hand and let him pull her up.

They walked in silence to the cafeteria. Stacey had her arms wrapped self-consciously around her chest the whole way. Because she'd been naked from using her dress as a tourniquet when the medics arrived, she had grabbed the first T-shirt and pair of jeans she found. The shirt, it turned out, didn't do much in the way of concealing what was beneath it, not without the normal undergarments. Jack had offered her his coat, but as Donny had so eloquently put it, he smelled like pickled diarrhea.

When they reached the vending machine, they got two cups of coffee and sat at a table in a secluded section of the room. Jack told her everything he'd been through, including everything Viktoriya had told him. He figured she'd find out from the FBI eventually, anyway.

Disbelief left her motionless. "My mother was KGB?"

Jack nodded. "I'm sorry. Is this too much right now? You've had a lot of curveballs thrown at you in the last two hours. I don't want to overload you."

She wiped a tear away and leaned back, trying to examine the last five years with this new knowledge as its decoder. "Seriously?"

"I think she blamed herself for what happened at the hotel. I'm sure she planned on following her orders before you were ever put in a compromising position."

She frowned. "Is that what you call it?"

Jack smiled. It was a good sign to see a hint of wit peeking through the pain. "But she never got an opportunity, and you were screwed."

She managed to laugh and reached across the table, hitting him on the arm.

"Ouch! Watch it. Your other husband beat the living crap out of me, remember?"

"You're not angry at me?"

He shrugged. "I'm not jumping for joy, but..." He touched the stitches above his right eye. "It is a better explanation than I expected. For a few minutes, I thought that maybe you wanted to get rid of me."

"Are you serious?"

"Just a few...tiny minutes."

She folded her arms on the table and grew serious. "Jack—"

He cut her off. "Listen, I'm just glad I didn't lose you. Whatever happened before is irrelevant. That little cheating on your husband with your husband thing... You did what you had to do to protect us. I'll get over it." Though saying it made him think about it, and thinking about it didn't make his voice all that convincing.

"What if I told you I didn't remember any of it? Or that he was terrible?"

"Would it be true?"

"How do I know? I was wasted the whole time."

They smiled, took a sip of coffee, and stared down at the table for a while.

"I'm so sorry about Donny and Ivan," she said.

Jack was, too, but again, the full realization of those losses was still busy forming out at sea. When it struck, it would be one brutal tempest, but for now he was too distracted by all the excitement and at having Stacey and Joseph back. He would deal with losing his friends soon enough. "Are you going to be okay?" he asked her.

She thought about it for a second, hooking a piece of hair behind an ear. "Yeah." She squinted. "What're we going to do? We don't have a house, right?"

"Don't worry about that. We'll figure it out once all this settles down. We'll be fine."

She thought about all he'd told her. "What about the CIA? Do you think they'll still try to..."

"Nah. The smartest thing for them to do is just leave it alone. The FBI might dig around and get close, but not close enough to make anyone sweat. I think if we keep quiet, if we let the FBI draw its own conclusions, then we'll be okay. The CIA won't want to bring unnecessary attention to this thing."

"There you are!"

The deep voice sounded from behind them, making them turn their heads. Joseph's doctor was walking briskly toward them, a small smile on his face. "You can see him now," he said once he was beside them.

Jack and Stacey jumped to their feet, locked hands, and followed the doctor. There was a lot they didn't know, and a lot they would probably never find out. There were still aspects of the story that didn't make much sense to Jack, but he was through thinking about it for now. All that mattered was Joseph—his son.

When they entered the recovery room, Joseph opened his eyes and smiled the most precious and heart-melting smile his parents had ever seen. His neck was wrapped, and he had some wires connecting him to machines, but other than that, he looked great.

"Hi, Mommy," he whispered. "Hi, Daddy." He lifted his hand and gave a tired wave.

They both sat down on the edge of the bed and tried their hardest to keep from smothering him with hugs and kisses.

Jack laid a hand on his tiny chest and smiled. "Hey, buddy. You okay?"

He tried nodding his head, but the wrappings made it impossible. "Yeah." Then he looked to his mother. "Is everything gonna be okay now?"

"Everything is gonna be okay now," she said.

28

THE NEW SAAB ROLLED to a stop before a wall of raked leaves that had been built at the top of the driveway. Jack stepped out of the car and was welcomed back to his new home by a brisk October 17 wind that pulled at his suit jacket and ruffled his hair.

Red-orange leaves snapped from the swaying branches above and whipped past him on the wings of some invisible current while dead leaves from the raked piles were summoned upward, twisting inside an eerie vortex. The image provoked thoughts of some time-traveling person from the future suddenly appearing naked in his front yard. But why a bodybuilding robot with an Austrian accent would show up at *his* house would be a complete mystery. Though he supposed it could be a Russian assassin finally coming after his family, using some secret teleporting technology. But that wouldn't make sense. Why would the Kremlin send an agent across the world to take them out now? The CIA, then? Or maybe the swirling leaves weren't indicative of a physical arrival but only a psychic one. A psychic assassin. He knew the government had them...

He turned his attention away from the leaves and looked up into the sky, satisfied that there wasn't a black hole forming in the clouds above his house. He would hate to have to move again. He jogged to the front door and looked across the street as he opened the front door. He could see the zipping clouds in the late-afternoon sky racing across the surface of the Delaware. It was strange being on this side of it now, the Jersey side.

"Joseph?" Jack called, closing the door on his imagination.

No answer.

"Mary?"

Mary was the babysitter, and the reason she was here today was because Stacey's company was running a huge event at Waterfront Park tonight. Some kind of Live Aid thing meant to raise awareness of the worldwide water crisis. A couple of actors, a Major League athlete, the entire cast of the Trenton Thunder, some politicians, and an author who'd written a book on the subject were all scheduled to speak between performances by some of the biggest names in music.

"Joseph! Mary!" He walked into the kitchen and tossed his keys onto the counter. He found a piece of notebook paper sitting on the kitchen table, big red letters scribbled across it.

Hey, Mr. Green. I talked to Mrs. Green and she said it was okay to take Joseph to see the four o' clock showing of that new Disney movie. Hope that's ok. Your phone wasn't on, so I left a message. —M

"Crap," Jack muttered, and he dug his cell out of his pocket. He'd forgotten to take it off silent after a meeting. Five missed calls. Two were from Mary, one was from Stacey, one was from someone at work, and one came from a blocked number. Three voicemails were waiting for him, and he listened to them while looking through the refrigerator for something to eat. His meeting had gone through lunch, and he was starving.

"Hi, Mr. Green, it's Mary. I've been trying to reach you, but I guess your phone's off. I called Mrs. Green and asked if I could take Joseph to the movies at four o' clock. She said it was okay as long as I promise to leave if he gets scared. So, I guess we'll be back around sixish. Bye!"

"End of message. To save this message, please—"

Jack deleted it.

"Next new message..."

He took out some lunchmeat and tossed it on the table.

"Hi, Jack. Things are pretty insane today..."

There was a long pause, and for a second, Jack thought the phone had shut off.

"—just know that I love you, okay? I miss you. Hey, maybe when I get home tonight..."

"End of message—message skipped. Next new message..."

He walked to the counter to grab the salt and pepper and noticed an unfamiliar book a few inches from where his keys had landed. The next message played.

"*The Donzerly Light*," he muttered out loud. And then he saw the author's name.

Ryne Douglas Pearson.

"Jack, it's Agent Johnson," the recorded voice said in his ear. Jack hadn't heard a peep from the FBI man since before the whole incident in Connecticut, not even during the ensuing investigation (though the investigation ended rather quickly, the headlines reading that Vadim had settled into a jealous rage, attacking his family when he learned of his wife's 'other' life with a secret husband—the missing doctor, the cruise, and the burning down of their house never being connected).

But Jack was focused on the book now. Slowly, he reached his trembling hand out and peeled back its cover. He didn't know what to expect, but part of him seemed to be preparing for a Polaroid of his family—Stacey, Joseph, and even the babysitter, all with some mortal wound, the book delivered from out of the vortex, the image time-stamped from some future date as a warning of what would happen if he ever decided to talk about things. But only the copyright information stared up at him.

Before he could stop himself, he was turning the book over and checking the back for a Russian note.

"...I think we should talk..." Agent Johnson said. *"...something hasn't been sitting right*

with me...”

Stacey liked the author, so what? He liked Pearson, too. He was just being paranoid.

“...we’re picking up some chatter...”

Thunder sounded outside, and a few raindrops splashed against the window that overlooked the backyard. If the coming storm didn’t pass quickly, the event at the park would be a washout, and all Stacey’s hard work would be for nothing.

“...we don’t think Vadim was the only person involved...”

Jack frowned, his attention tripping over the voice. What was Johnson saying?

“...Vadim didn’t write the notes in the book...”

A bolt of lightning tore through the sky.

Jack was confused. What was the FBI still doing looking at this? He thought the CIA had shut them down. What was Johnson up to?

“...I’ll call you back when I have more information. But keep your eyes open, Jack.”

“End of—Message saved. No new messages. First skip—”

He hung up just as another call was coming in. Stacey.

“Hello?”

"Hi, babe, it's me. Where you been all day?"

"Had my phone on silent for a meeting. Looks like you might get rained out."

"Yeah, the sky doesn't look too promising. Guess maybe we forgot to pay our HAARP bill. Did you get Mary's message?"

"Yeah."

"Okay. Did you get mine?" There was innuendo wrapped around her tone.

"Yeah."

"I may need you tonight. Be ready, okay? It's been a crappy day."

His eyes fell to the book. "What's *Donzerly Light*?"

"What?" she asked.

"There's a book here on the counter by Ryne Douglas Pearson. *The Donzerly Light*."

There was a pause on her end.

"Hello?" he asked.

"Oh, the book! Sorry, babe. Does that bother you? I'll totally get rid of it if it does. You know I just like the author."

"What does it mean?"

"What does what mean?"

"The title, *Donzerly Light*."

Another pause. *"I'm not sure. I haven't started it yet. Why?"*

"Just curious."

"You okay?"

"Yeah. You?"

"I will be. Once I'm back in bed with you. I love you, Jack. No matter what, I'll always love you."

"I love you, too. See you when you get back. Good luck."

They hung up.

Jack stared out into the backyard. Something about her word choice seemed oddly cryptic. And he wasn't referring to the implied night of passion. "Oh, shut up, Jerry."

He walked to the den with a sandwich in his hands, trying to shrug off the question of why Johnson would call now after three months of complete silence.

He sat before the television and took a quick note of the framed Bible verse hanging on the wall above it. *Love believes all things, hopes all things...* It was the same one that Grandmom had, and Stacey had even let him hang it up without a fight. He still couldn't believe that.

He let his eyes descend to the TV as he flipped on *SportsCenter*, and he became immediately inundated with more conversation about the upcoming Monday night game. He took a bite of his dinner and tried to lose the pursuing thoughts through a maze of sports talk. But he couldn't escape it. *The Donzerly Light* by

Pearson and a phone call from Agent Johnson all within a matter of minutes? Jerry didn't believe in coincidences. He listened to Johnson's message more closely.

When the message was over, he ended the connection and tossed the phone onto the coffee table in front of him. He didn't understand the source of Johnson's concern. Hadn't they known from the beginning that the handwriting in the novels didn't match the handwriting in the letters? *So why...* And then that little fact dropped into place like a coin in a jukebox, playing lyrics that Jack had never stopped to consider before. Stacey had told him right there in the hospital three months ago that the books came from Vadim. So if Vadim didn't write the notes... But who else could the books be from? And how could he not have seen this hole in the story before? Because he didn't want to, of course.

He got up off the couch, now completely oblivious to whatever was going on in the NFL, and sat down at the computer. He pulled up Amazon and checked all prior orders. *Donzerly* hadn't come from Amazon. He then checked all their credit card accounts and found nothing recent that would suggest a possible book purchase. Next he checked PayPal and their debit card. Nothing. That left cash, so he looked up the phone numbers to all the nearest bookstores and asked if they carried the book. None of them did.

So someone (not Vadim, he was dead) had given the book to her. He was pretty sure that Stacey had implied two things on the phone just now: *she* had the book because *she* liked the author and that *he* might not like it because *he* would relate it to Vadim.

He swore, got a beer from the refrigerator, and returned to the television.

SINKING. MOONLIGHT GROWING FAINTER and fainter beneath a dark curtain, lungs on fire...

He always woke up at that moment, right before he could pass out from holding his breath so long. With a lungful of precious air now, he looked around the room and was satisfied that he'd been dreaming. The nightmare just wouldn't leave him alone, and he wished he could punch Mr. Sandman in the face. He moved his feet onto the floor and held his head in his hands. As the ocean's depths receded, he was left with the remnants of some mystery he'd been troubled by before falling overboard again. It was knocking on the door of consciousness. Robots from the future wanted to kidnap Joseph? No, that wasn't it. Then what was this feeling? Why was he sure something was wrong? Russian assassins? Psychic warfare?

And it came back—the book, Johnson's call, his conversation with Stacey...

The front door opened, and banter between Mary and Joseph came drifting into the den. Jack looked at the clock on the wall and saw that it was 7:08.

"Hi, Daddy!" Joseph shouted. His smiling face rounded the corner.

"Hey, buddy. The movie good?"

"Yeah! It was awesome!" he shouted. He threw a fist in the air and jumped, kicking his legs up and under him. Other than an occasional bad dream, he'd made a remarkable recovery, and it sometimes seemed that the white scar across his neck was the only evidence of that day's trauma.

Mary smiled patiently. She wanted to be paid so that she could go straight back to the mall, where her friends were already waiting for her.

"Thank you, Mary." He pulled out his wallet and extracted a few bills. "Here you go."

"Thanks, Mr. Green." She turned to Joseph. "See ya later, squirt."

"Bye!" Joseph hollered.

She turned, waved, and left.

Joseph was already out of the room and halfway up the stairs by the time the door banged shut, and Jack had to chase after him. "What do you want for dinner, Joe?"

"Pizza!" he hollered back before closing the door to his room.

"Okay, fifteen minutes!" Jack went back to the kitchen to throw a frozen pizza into the oven. It was 7:13.

Stacey's event was scheduled to start at 7:30, so he switched the television to the appropriate channel while the pizza thawed in the oven. *Who is supposed to sing the national anthem?* he wondered. He punched buttons on the remote. Simon somebody. *Simple Simon?* No, that was the Pearson book.

The books...

He turned them over in his mind, sifting Stacey's lie through mental fingers. *The Donzerly Light...* Why did that sound so familiar?

Before he knew it, the oven was beeping, and it snapped him away from his pondering. He called Joseph down.

After making a sliding entrance across the kitchen floor in his socks, Joseph seamlessly transitioned onto a chair at the table. He had half a cheesy triangle in his mouth before Jack could even sit down.

Jack ruffled his son's hair and then turned his attention back to the living room, to the event that was about to take place on the television.

Donzerly Light. He couldn't shake the title, the feeling that he should know something about it. He said it out loud. "Donzerly Light."

"What did you say?" Joseph asked through the tendrils of melted cheese hanging from his mouth.

He broke it up into syllables. "Don-zer-ly-light."

"Are you okay, Daddy-o?" Joseph asked, giggling.

Don-zer-ly light...

He grabbed the book and sat at the table next to Joseph. He skimmed through the first few chapters in search of something that might explain its title.

Bingo. Right there in chapter one.

When he was younger, it said, the main character always thought the lyrics to the national anthem were actually "by the donzerly light."

The national anthem.

And in fact, the singer—the Simon someone, who was actually a woman—was about to kick off Stacey's event. *What the heck is her name?* She was somewhat of a political voice, an activist when it came to things like poverty, AIDS, starvation, human trafficking. She was Bono working on a bigger scale but without the legendary acclaim. And then the bottom of the screen solved his little puzzle before his memory could. Rose Simon. He snapped his fingers.

"You're silly, Daddy. You're a silly monkey!" Joseph laughed, chomping away at another slice.

The wind blew Rose Simon's hair back over her shoulders as she smiled up at the packed stadium and the clouds beyond. She brought the microphone to her lips and began.

A collage of panning and zooming angle shots faded in and out over her face while she sang, giving a live soundtrack to the editor's representation of the stadium—the stage erected between first and third base, the crowd, the banners (decorated by a pair of children's hands reaching up for falling water) flapping in the wind, the American flag atop the stadium...

Jack's phone rang.

Blocked number.

He swore, to which Joseph began crossing his fingers at him and shaking his head with disapproval.

"Sorry," Jack whispered.

"Jack, it's Johnson. Did you get my message?"

"Yeah. What's going on? I thought—"

"Just listen. There's someone else."

"What are you talking about?"

"Vadim was just meant to be the fall guy."

"Yeah, we knew that already."

"No." He sighed, and Jack could tell he was guarding his words over the phone. *"This has nothing to do with the Agency."*

Jack's back straightened. "I haven't heard from you since you left me standing in the mountains. Why are you calling me now?"

"The books didn't come from Vadim."

"You knew that already. The handwriting in the books was different than in the letters."

"Yeah, but we didn't know what it meant until now. Who the books were from..."

Rose Simon's powerful voice belting out the words "*...BYYY THE DAWWWWN'S EARRRRLYYYY LIIIIIIGHT*" lifted his eyes to the television. She smiled as the crowd cheered, waving—

There was a flash, a broken, pixilated mess of colors splashed across the screen, and then big multicolored bars standing alone in the sudden silence of the den.

"...there may still be something in play..." Johnson was saying. *"But not orchestrated from our end..."*

Jack's hands were shaking, his eyes pulled into a trance by the colors, and he could vaguely make out Joseph's voice inquiring about the TV being broken. The world tightened on him, squeezing him between the puzzle pieces that were just now falling into place. "I have to go," he mumbled into the phone. He ended the call and let his arm swing limp to his side.

The books.

The House of Thunder. October's Ghost. Seventeen Moments of Spring. Simple Simon. The Donzerly Light.

As far as he knew, the last two had no Soviet plotlines. But it didn't matter. The meaning was now clear enough. Bile rose in his throat, and he was falling from the ship all over again, his world inverted and upside down, everything uncertain.

The House of Thunder: Waterfront Park, home of the Trenton Thunder.

October's Ghost and *Seventeen Moments of Spring*: October 17.

Simple Simon and *The Donzerly Light*: Rose Simon singing the National Anthem.

Jack shouted an obscenity. Joseph's eyes went wide with shock, his pizza frozen in space halfway to his mouth. "Daddy!" he cried out.

Jack ignored him and walked to the TV. He flipped to a news station. Waited.

Five minutes later, the reports were pouring in.

An explosion at Waterfront Park.

So many thoughts rammed their way into Jack's mind. All of them seemed to make sense at first but then fell away to nothing the next moment. His suspicion was that Stacey was somehow involved. His fear was that she was not.

He dialed her number.

No answer.

He tried again.

"Hi."

"Stacey!" he yelled, overjoyed that she was alive.

"Did you see it on TV?" Her voice sounded strangely detached. Shock, maybe.

"The broadcast went down. I saw a flash of light. The news is reporting an explosion. Are you okay?"

Joseph began whimpering in the background, and Jack turned to form the soundless words with his lips. “It’s okay.”

“Yeah, I’m okay. I’m coming home.”

“How bad is it?”

“I don’t know. I didn’t really see...”

“What do you mean you didn’t see?”

“I’m on my way home now. I love you.”

The call ended.

Jack stared at the phone. The conversation didn’t make any sense to him. She must be in shock. And then he realized she could be wandering the streets, confused, a piece of home plate in her back.

Or...

No, he wouldn’t let himself think that. He couldn’t. *She* couldn’t.

But there it was. *The Donzerly Light*. Sitting right on the countertop.

29

JACK WAS SITTING IN a chair beside the bed, rocking back and forth, waiting. A streetlamp that was casting its light through an open window outlined the room's contents with a faint yellowish glow.

Sixty thousand people...

That was how many people could have been killed at Stacey's event tonight, though the last report he'd seen estimated the casualties to be somewhere below fifty. They were attributing the low number to the work of an amateur.

Staring into the darkness, he absentmindedly turned the *Donzerly Light* over in his hands again. Stacey had a lot of explaining to do. Whatever she was involved with, he would know tonight.

No more secrets. Yet, he didn't really want to know, did he? What if his love for her wasn't strong enough to survive the truth? What would they do? What about Joseph? Would he do whatever was necessary to keep his home intact? Even if she had something to do with what happened tonight? *Love believes all things, hopes all things...*

He moved his eyes to the invisible pictures that once hung on their bedroom walls, imagining that this bedroom was their old one. He studied the framed image of Grandmom from memory. Then he moved on to the others, recalling every one of their details. Some of the photos held pictures of Ivan and Donny, but right now it was the family pictures that were being analyzed in the headquarters of his mind. Their wedding, summer and winter vacations, Joseph's birthdays. He wondered about the truth of them.

Johnson didn't think this was an inside job orchestrated by a faction of the US government to instigate another war. He thought it was a genuine attack. But by... Russia? Why would Russia blow up an event aimed at supplying water to the waterless? If Russia wanted a war with the United States, wouldn't they just shoot a few nukes over and get the whole thing rolling? Unless they were waving some Muslim terrorist group's flag, intending to draw the US deeper into the Middle East so that they could sneak through the back door while the country had its head stuck down the War on Terror toilet.

The sound of a car pulling into the driveway brought a halt to his conjecture. Stacey was home. And after doors opened and closed, her padded steps could be heard ascending the stairs.

His heart beat fast.

She stepped into the doorway, and the dim light from the window painted her figure as a dark silhouette.

"Hi," she said.

"Hi."

She stepped into the bedroom and began undressing.

Jack watched her shape dance beneath the shadows. "What're you doing?" he asked softly.

"Getting ready for bed." She flung her shoes across the floor toward the closet.

"Are you hurt?"

"No."

He reached over and turned the bedside lamp on. A soft glow washed over the room. "You look okay." Her clothes didn't even appear dirty.

She unbuttoned her shirt but didn't answer. Then she pulled it off.

"The dawn's early light?" he asked, holding the book up so that she could see it.

Stacey looked at her husband and, for a second, feigned confusion. "What's wrong, Jack?" The tone in her voice indicated an attempt to understand why he wasn't embracing her, kissing her, glad she was okay. But only for a second.

"Is it just a coincidence?"

"Is what a coincidence?"

"*The House of Thunder, Seventeen Days of Spring, October's Ghost, Simple Simon, The Donzerly Light*? What is this, Stacey? Or Anna. Or whatever the hell your name is. I know the books weren't from Vadim."

She sighed, shimmied out of her dress pants, and stood tall in her underwear. "Is Joseph asleep?"

"Probably."

She sat down on the edge of the bed, facing him.

"You put the book there because you wanted me to find it, didn't you? You wanted me to put it all together..."

She shook her head. "I didn't put the book there. It's not mine."

"You said you liked the author, that you hadn't started reading it yet..." He was growing impatient.

"I didn't want to worry you."

"*Worry* me?" he asked in disbelief.

"I tried to stop him," she whispered, her eyes suddenly far off.

"Who?"

She met his gaze, and a tear fell from one of her eyes. It caught the light and sparkled like a diamond down her cheek. "I should have told you before, but..." A hand went to her mouth. It was trembling.

"Tell me now."

"I couldn't before. He would've known, and..." She looked away. "I thought I'd be able to stop him if he ever went through with it."

"I need answers, Stacey. Right now."

She looked hurt by the coldness in his voice but nodded her consent. "You're right. The books were never from Vadim. I lied about that."

"What were they?"

"Codes. Messages. His way of communicating."

Jack leaned forward. "The text you got on the boat that night..."

She nodded. "He developed a number system to use for the books he chose. He got a kick out of finding titles that, when put together, would spell out his plan. I think he thought he was taunting the authorities, hiding the details of the mission right under their noses, as if they should've been able to piece it all together and prevent it. He was a lunatic, thriving in his own lunatic logic. He sent many books just in case someone was watching, but only the books with relevant titles were decipherable."

"Who's '*he*'?"

She sat up straight, summoning the strength to finally lay everything bare. After a deep breath, she began. "You know about my father and mother."

He nodded and leaned back, settling into the chair while trying to prepare himself for what was going to be another backhanded slap to everything he knew about their life. What did Jesus say about being struck on the cheek? Turn the other one also? Well, here it was. Round two. He'd gotten over the first, but as he watched the windup of the second, he knew that what was coming now might not be as salvageable.

"I figured out that my mother was KGB when I was seventeen. I didn't know anything about it other than the movies I'd seen, didn't really know anything about Russia. But I decided that I wanted to follow in my parents' footprints, to make them proud. I didn't think my mother would allow it, though, so I kept my plans to myself. My sophomore year of college, I got a chance to go to Russia." She moved her head toward the window.

Jack didn't know she'd been to Russia. If she knew Viki was KGB, then she had been pretending to be surprised by his telling her in the hospital.

"That's where I met Vadim," she said.

"You met him in Russia?"

"Yeah." She laughed, but it was mostly in disgust. "I was taken with him. He was an agent just like my father. He'd gone to school in the US, and he was about to be sent back as a plant. He said he wanted to stay in touch. We did." Her eyes shifted back to her feet. "The excitement of being married to a spy wore off pretty quick. He was an angry, violent man. Like I told you before, I wanted out. I wanted what all my friends in college were striving for, a house, the loving husband, kids, a career..."

Jack could see the truth on her face. Viktoriya had at least gotten that much right.

"There was another guy in Russia. His name was Fedyenka Yevstigneyev."

"The books were from him?"

She nodded. "He was infatuated with me, but I could tell right away that he was too fanatical. His ideas were..." She bit her lip. "He really scared me." She stood and removed her bra. Then she walked to the closet, opened the doors, and pulled a nightgown off a hanger. She raised her arms and let it fall down over her head. It fell elegantly over her accented figure like a coating of silk paint.

"He resented that I chose Vadim over him," she continued, "but he didn't let it interfere with our work."

"Your work..."

"We were working on a plot that would bring the US into a war with Russia." She shook her head. "I never really thought it would go anywhere. I really didn't want to see America destroyed, let alone play a part in it. I was just playing a game. But by the time I actually grew up and understood what I was into, I was in too deep to just say goodbye. It's why they had me become an event planner, for god's sake." She looked him in the eyes. "I thought Vadim and I were just fooling around—"

Jack sneered. "Yeah, he seemed to me like the kind of guy who would joke around about stuff like that."

She ignored him. "Fedyenka was different. He was insane. He started making advances on me once he discovered my unhappiness with Vadim. He said he would have me, and that he wouldn't take no for an answer this time, that I'd made a mistake in choosing Vadim over him before. From then on, he started setting Vadim up as his scapegoat, everything he planned leading back to him. And he finally gave him up to the CIA."

Jack felt like he should be taking notes.

"I was overjoyed, though, when the CIA turned Vadim. It gave me a chance to finally get away." More lip chewing. "I told you that part."

Jack couldn't believe that the woman he'd shared the last five years with, and the most intimate experiences that could be had in life—marriage, the birth and raising of a child, *family*—had been carrying this secret past with her the entire time. But he tried to withhold complete sympathy until her timeline caught up with tonight. To the bomb.

"I wanted a life with you, to bury all that stuff in some black hole somewhere. I didn't want anything to do with the SVR, Russia, any of it. And for an entire year it seemed like I got my wish. I hadn't heard from Vadim—he didn't even know my new name or where I was—and I hadn't gotten anything from Fedyenka."

"Until your mother was activated again."

She nodded. "I didn't know she was supposed to kill him, that that's why she told him where I was."

Jack held up a hand, pausing her story. "Is Joseph really my son?"

A hint of disapproval crossed her face. "You don't see it? He's more you than me."

"But is he more *Vadim* than me?"

"Oh, please." She smiled sheepishly. "Jack, he's *our* son. I told you I'd show you the test results."

He hated the fact that she'd needed a test to determine who Joseph's father was, but he was learning to get over it, so... moving on. "Yeah, yeah, yeah...you had to pleasure your other husband for a while. I know that part, too. And then?"

She frowned. "I was able to get out of that mess without telling him my new name or where I was. But a few months later, Fedyenka found me. I told him to stay the hell away from me, but he threatened to tell Vadim about you. I told him I'd tell Vadim that he sold him out to the CIA. And he said he'd kill you and cut the baby out of my stomach as he raped me."

That was actually a pretty disturbing image, and if Jack had the chance, he'd kill the psycho just for uttering it. "Did you—"

"He didn't want me like that anymore. I was the event planner. He needed me to help set up his event. That's when the books started."

"The messages didn't sound like some psycho who was ready to kill you for rejecting him."

"He was mocking me. I don't know. I stopped trying to make sense of him a long time ago."

"And the books were to be translated according to his code?"

"Yes. When the SVR got wind of Vadim being turned, and I guess after my mother failed to eliminate him, they began feeding him false information. But then, when it looked like the CIA was planning on using him as a patsy for some kind of false flag, the SVR activated my mother again, not giving her the option to fail this time. But Fedyenka saw the false flag as a golden opportunity and made sure everything he did could be covered beneath its umbrella. He had Vadim as a patsy twice over."

"But then your mom kills Vadim."

"No. Then you survive and get the FBI involved. Which makes the CIA eventually scrap the op. But Fedyenka had planned for that and was still proceeding with his own attack, still setting up Vadim as the fall guy."

"And then Vadim is killed."

"And he needs another patsy."

He felt the realization run over his brain like melting ice, cold understanding dripping into his eyes and clearing his vision. "You."

"When you told me about the *Donzerly* book, I knew he'd been in our house. That he was setting me up."

"What was he trying to accomplish by blowing up an event about water?"

"A war that would revive the Soviet Union and make Russia the world's primary superpower."

"He thought Russia could win that war?"

"With everything he was. He was a rogue agent, though. Nothing he was doing came down from the chain of command. He took it upon himself to instigate a war, to get the show on the road. He didn't care who started the war, as long as there was one. There are parties on both sides, it seems, that want to get the whole thing over with."

"But why *this* event?"

"I got him to believe that I was totally on board with his plan, and I suggested something that would really stir the American public into action. The kind of impulsive action that would make everyone too angry to think things through. The need to go kill someone. Anyone. Like after 9/11. Like the first Gulf War. Just like Americans wouldn't tolerate that 'babies being thrown from incubators' fiction, neither would they tolerate something like this."

Jack's head spun. "This was *your* idea?"

"I needed to stop him. And the best shot I had was letting him go through with it. It was risky, but it was the only way I could be sure he wouldn't come after our family, or that he wouldn't try blowing something else up later on."

He rubbed his forehead, trying to massage understanding into his brain. He watched Stacey's lower lip begin to tremble.

"But I couldn't get to the last two bombs in time," she whispered.

His wife racing around a stadium trying to deactivate bombs before they could detonate? Who was this woman?

Who had he married? "What about Fedyenka?"

"When you mentioned the book, I knew he was planning on pinning the whole thing on me. I don't even know how he was planning on doing that, or how it would appear that Russia was behind it. But I had the drop on him. I hit him in the back of the head with a fire extinguisher."

"And...he's dead?" He almost wished he wasn't so that he could do the honors himself.

"I hit him a lot."

Jack turned her tale over in his head, searching for a crack or fissure that would topple the whole story. When he couldn't find one, he asked, "So is it done now?"

She managed a small, pleading smile that barely made it through her mask of exhaustion. "I guess that depends on you."

The puzzle pieces were spinning too violently for him to place them in their right and proper places. The storm would have to run its course before he could effectively connect all the dots and decide whether or not he believed her story. Right now...he just didn't know. She'd lied to him before. He was angry and sad, but he was relieved that she was okay. He didn't know what that meant. Regardless of her motive, she'd helped plan an attack that killed up to fifty innocent people.

Stacey climbed into bed and pulled the covers up to her shoulders. Tears trickled onto the pillows.

Jack just stared at her.

What was he supposed to do? Make a citizen's arrest? Call the cops? The FBI? Homeland? What about Joseph? Could he live with himself if he chose to forget it? Even if an investigation didn't lead to Stacey, would they really be able to move on?

Stacey closed her eyes and said softly, "I'm sorry. For everything. You deserve so much more than this." And then she opened her eyes and looked at him. "I want you to do whatever you think is right. If you have to turn me in, then turn me in." She paused. "But there's something you should know first."

"What?"

"We're having another baby."

JACK SAT AT THE kitchen table. His fifth cup of coffee was resting between his hands and sending wisps of steam floating upward. He'd wanted alcohol but was able to resist the urge, knowing that he needed to stay as sharp as possible. To think through this whole mess with a sound mind.

After Stacey fell asleep, Jack had sat there next to the bed, watching her until the early hours of the morning. The slap she'd delivered proved to be a padded one. And while it spun his head and dizzied his senses, it was not the blow of betrayal and mass murder that he had feared. Staring at her that long brought back shared memories that would always be precious to him, and he realized that he wanted to believe her.

As the storm clouds piled up in the sky above the house and rain began to fall, Jack wondered what purpose she would have to lie now? With Viktoriya dead, Vadim dead, and this other guy dead, she could've left last night, disappeared into another identity after the explosion. He guessed that she could've just come back for Joseph, and that she could have him thrown off another boat as soon as possible. Maybe she was a Russian plant and this was her cover all along. Maybe her mission had been to stop Fedyenka, a rogue agent operating according to his own volition. Maybe she was CIA and the whole thing was more complicated and twisted than he could ever understand. How could he ever really know?

He could get in touch with Johnson, but if Stacey was telling the truth, then he would have exposed her background to the FBI for nothing. Then she'd probably end up being *their* patsy for some future plot.

It was these thoughts, and scores like them, that prevented him from falling asleep. Instead, as thunder sounded, he'd gone downstairs and started on the coffee.

And there he still sat; only now he was watching Stacey and Joseph in the room across from him. They were tickling each other, laughing, and running around, morphing continuously into a wide variety of animals. Joseph's adoration for his mother was unmistakable, pure joy beaming in his eyes as they regarded her. How could Jack ever take that away from his son? How could he put his son through what he'd experienced at six years old? No, he *needed* to believe her, for Joseph's sake if not for his own.

But that wasn't even the most influential component helping make up his mind. The biggest nail pinning his verdict to the courtroom door was the stunning revelation that his wife was expecting again. Whether she was telling the whole truth and nothing but the truth suddenly became inconsequential. What was he going to do, deliver his pregnant wife to the CIA? Condemn the woman carrying his child to some black site to be waterboarded, the rest of her life spent in a secret prison somewhere? Would the child be presented to him at the Pentagon, a flag-swaddled gesture of good faith on behalf of a forgiving nation? Not likely.

Love believes all things, hopes all things, endures *all things.*

He sipped more coffee. He hadn't spoken to her yet today, but they'd made eye contact a few times, and she seemed to know that he really didn't have a choice now that his unborn child was part of the equation. Maybe that had been her plan, her security net, her assurance that he wouldn't turn her over. He might never know for sure, but he was throwing all his chips down on love and hoping for the best. There was no other option, was there?

He stood and made his way into the living room.

Stacey watched him curiously as he approached. When he sat down on the floor beside her, putting his arm around her shoulders and kissing her lightly on the cheek, she asked, "So is this goodbye or hello?"

Joseph jumped in his lap, and he tousled his hair. "You lied to me twice, three strikes and you're out."

"I'll hit this one out of the park, I swear." She smiled. "I love you, Jack. I always have. You know that's why I never told you anything, right? To protect you? To keep you?"

He took her hand. "We'll take it from here." And then he paused. "Under one condition."

"Anything."

"You quit your job. No more event planning, no more anything. Stay here with the kids."

"Deal."

"And I want the whole story. Step by step. There are still some holes that I need filled." And indeed there was. One of them was the books. Who wanted them? Was it the CIA that burnt down his house like Johnson thought, or was it Fedyenka reclaiming his books and collecting Vadim's letters in order to properly make Vadim out to be the fall guy? Were the books and letters meant to be saved and later planted or destroyed with certainty? He would ask her later. But not now.

"Okay."

And though he knew the happiness was slightly exaggerated beneath all the unasked questions and the shadows of doubt that still lurked within their house, he thought back to when he was sinking in the middle of the ocean and the three things his mind fixated on in the face of certain death. Stacey. Joseph. God. And though the last of the three was vague and still needed some pursuing, the first two were not. They were everything to him and always would be. The coming months wouldn't be easy, but he was jumping in with both feet, perfectly aware that no ship would be coming back for him this time. This was it. He was giving himself to her, pledging his trust to her.

He hoped it was the right decision. He hoped Grandmom was right.

LATER THAT NIGHT, THEY watched as the corporate news channels and the White House all blamed some new Bin Laden for the attack. They were already talking about more police state legislation needing to be passed and that more troops should be sent somewhere fast. No one knew where exactly, but everyone assumed the same thing. Some windbags on certain "news" channels were already calling for a nuclear strike on Iran.

"Well," Stacey said, "looks like everyone's getting what they wanted out of this anyway."

Jack nodded. "They'll finally get their war with Iran, and they'll torch the Constitution for more Patriot Acts..."

"Every American family will probably be assigned a live-in TSA agent."

"Oh, man, that would suck."

"And you, *Jerry*, will be named an enemy of the state and executed for treason by a new division of thought police."

"Think I'll be in Canada by the time that happens."

"Still part of the NAU. There's no getting away now, my love. Agent Johnson's probably turning you in as we speak."

He frowned. "You're right. Russia gets more time to prepare as we jump into another war. We're the Soviets fighting Afghanistan, and they're just waiting until we're spread so thin and fighting so many wars... It might as well have been a false-flag attack by both sides. They both got what they wanted out of it."

She picked up the remote and shut off the war propaganda. She leaned into him and kissed him.

He thought that he would resist any type of intimacy for a while, but he found himself leaning into her kiss, everything that had happened in the last few months suddenly gone. Thrown overboard, stories of cancer, missing doctors, murdered friends, burnt-down houses, false-flag operations, other husbands... It was all a dream, and her kiss had finally awakened him from it.

If only that were so, he thought, Ivan, Donny, and even Viktoriya flashing in his mind.

But soon Stacey had his mind off them, too, and Jack could only hope that there would be no masked men waking him up this time.

Love believes all things, hopes all things, endures all things...

"Amen," he muttered.

Stacey smiled at him.

30

CHRISTMAS HAD BEEN wonderful, and two days later, the magic of it was still lingering in the air. Clumps of torn wrapping paper were scattered around the house, still resting where they'd landed after the paper fight that ensued after every opened present. Jack could see one in the Christmas tree, a shot from Stacey that he'd had to duck to avoid. There was another one on top of the fireplace, one resting on the back of the couch, and a rather large one stuck above the window, wedged between the wall and the curtain rod. What a blast the day had been. Stacey had summoned him into the kitchen a couple of times for some special mommy and daddy time while Joseph beheld his new presents with wide-eyed wonder.

Jack was putting together one of those new presents now—a *Star Wars*-themed bicycle. He'd already lost the assembly directions, but he didn't need them. He'd put together enough bikes in his day. He worked the wrench and screwdriver as quietly as he could. It was almost midnight and he didn't want to wake anyone. Joseph was sleeping in his bed next to his new favorite new toys, and Stacey had slipped into a deep sleep about forty-five minutes ago after some more mommy and daddy time. He, himself, had been unable to sleep and, after staring at the ceiling for twenty minutes, decided to come down here. He put on a pot of coffee, turned on his favorite independent radio station, plugged the Christmas lights back in, and pulled the bike out of its box.

The radio was turned low, but Jack could still hear it over his work. He hadn't listened to much of the news since the Waterfront Park event. He was afraid of what they might uncover, that their investigation might lead back to Stacey, and ignorance on that front was bliss. But tonight, his "Jerry" itch was back. Not necessarily about that night, but about everything else going on in the world.

But, unfortunately, all they were still talking about was that night.

He was about to walk over and switch to some Christmas music when a caller came on the line.

"*I work for the Federal Bureau of Investigation,*" a male voice stated immediately.

The host paused. "*Can we have your name, sir?*"

"*No.*"

"*How are we supp—*"

"*Just listen. You're right about the CIA covering up what really happened at Waterfront Park.*"

Jack froze.

"*You mean it was an inside job?*" the host asked.

"*They found the bomber in the rubble. They lied about that.*"

He slowly stood.

The self-professed FBI man continued, "*He was found with a bullet in his head.*"

Wrong. Stacey had beaten the guy with a fire extinguisher. This guy was just some crank.

The host seemed dubious as well. "*You're telling me that the CIA is hiding the identity of the bomber?*"

"*Last week, police found the body of a doctor who had been missing since July. He was shot to death. The ballistics report shows that he was killed by the same gun that killed the bomber."*

All the yuletide glee Jack was reveling in vanished in an instant.

"*What's the connection?*" the host pressed.

"*I don't know. It's being covered up. But the bomber had a gun on him, too. And that gun was used in the murder of a Russian American named Ivan Alvang.*"

"Ivan..." Jack whispered. He stepped closer to the speakers.

The host of the news show asked the caller if he had any proof.

"*None that I can get my hands on. Listen, you know how these things work. I'm just trying to give your audience a clue. You guys do what you do with it. The official story will start to unravel beneath these questions.*"

"*Why are you doing this?*"

The caller fell silent. "*Because I lost someone close to me, and I owe it to him to expose the truth.*"

Jack stared at the radio as the voice rolled around the rim of his mind over and over again. It dropped in at the buzzer.

Johnson.

Jack's heart was pounding in his chest, everything he made himself believe over the last months falling to pieces in the face of this revelation.

Johnson's now-familiar voice said, "*Start with that.*" And he hung up.

Jack didn't hear what the host was saying now. His mind was too busy digging up all the lies. And then something that Stacey said to him on the boat dropped into his memory like a bomb and blew everything he believed into a million pieces.

Don't worry about it, honey. If truth be told, I caught you.

He noticed a distinct shadow on the wall in front of him.

His heart stopped in his chest.

He moved his gaze to one of the red balls hanging on the Christmas tree beside him and saw Stacy's pregnant figure in its reflection.

She reached over and turned the radio off.

Excerpt From Man In The Woods

JACK GREEN STOOD IN the driveway behind the black RAV4 and stared at the backup plan he'd packed into the trunk. Two coolers filled with food and drink, two duffel bags of clothes, and another bag of random items he thought they might want in the event things went sideways (and if he was honest with himself, he was sort of hoping they would). He went down his mental checklist one last time. Most of the stuff he wouldn't need. Maybe none of it. But it was always better to be looking at it than for it.

Satisfied, he closed the trunk and turned. Leaned against the bumper. As he watched the mid-June sun dip beneath the horizon, he checked his new watch.

8:34 on Sunday. He worked the buttons on the side and set an alarm for 7p.m. He'd want to keep in mind what time the sun set while they were out there, and he thought an hour and a half reminder should be enough to wrap up whatever it was they might find themselves in the middle of.

The urge to smoke struck him like a freight train, and he frowned. He'd taken up the habit about a year after the cruise ship incident when a guy at a bar had offered him one of his cigarettes. He then spent the next three years wishing he'd turned it down. But he eventually overcame the habit and could only hope he'd stopped in time to avoid any long-term damage. He wanted to be around for any grandchildren. Plus, the fact that secondhand smoke racked up more victims per year than gun violence sort of made him feel like a dick. So wanting one now, seemingly out of nowhere, was interesting.

He went inside.

HE WALKED INTO THE kitchen and stood at the table. Stacey was in front of the stove, her back to him. He stared at her, studying her figure as she sipped from a wineglass, her mind somewhere else. She still looked great, and though there were times he missed her blond hair, he liked her as a brunette even more. He loved the way she was wearing it now. Long, down her back, the blond highlights like feathered flames. She knew he loved her hair like that, and after being married for more than a decade, he was pretty certain what it meant. He looked at his watch again and decided that he'd better finish up. He sure didn't want to run out of time.

She turned, leaned against the stove, and tilted her head. "Almost done?" she asked, taking another sip.

He nodded. "Think so." Yup, there was no doubt about where this was going. Hair + wine + questions about bedtime + trip tomorrow morning = some mommy and daddy alone time.

She pushed off the oven and walked to the table. She looked down at the equipment that covered it and smiled.

"What?" he asked.

She picked up the survival guide he'd ordered a few months ago and flipped through the pages. "Nothing."

He snatched the book out of her hands.

"That's a lot of underlining," she said.

"I'm like Anthony Hopkins in *The Edge*." He tapped the side of his head. "It's all up here now."

"Mmm...book smarts in the wilderness. What could go wrong?" Another sip. "Why are you taking it if it's all—" she tapped her head in mock fashion "—up here?"

"Because I might forget which berries nourish you and which ones kill you."

"You definitely don't want to mix up your berries."

"I sure don't."

"Could ruin the week."

"Could ruin my colon." He sighed. "I hate the woods."

Stacey looked toward the steps in the other room. "Shhh..."

"I know. I know. Boy would be searching the classifieds for a new father before breakfast if he heard me say that."

"Think you can fake it?"

Her question, as innocent as it was, touched an old nerve, and he had to bite his tongue to keep from responding with some smart-ass comment.

She seemed to notice but didn't say anything, and the moment passed just as they always had over the last eight years. So much subtext. So much innuendo. So many elephants in the house. But it was their unspoken agreement not to drudge up the past that had allowed them to keep moving forward.

She walked around the table and kissed him. "Don't stay up too late. There's something I want to give you before you go."

"Should only be a few more minutes."

She walked out of the room.

He scratched his unshaven face as he swept his eyes over the stuff scattered across the table. Then he turned and looked into the living room, at the stuff he had piled on the floor in there too. He checked his watch again. He figured he had a half-hour window before Stacey fell asleep and he missed out on whatever it was she had for him. He got to work.

First, he picked up the knife. Held it up to the light.

Everything he'd read said that the belt knife was the most vital tool because it could be used to recreate most other things. It was recommended that it be kept on your person at all times, preferably in a leather sheath with a flap that snapped shut over the handle. Leather because whatever lubricant was used to protect the knife from rusting would end up in the leather and be applied to the blade whenever it was inserted. The downside was that leather held water when it got wet. Which was why he'd followed someone's suggestion and waterproofed it by soaking the sheath in olive oil, letting it drip dry over the last twenty-four hours. Stacy had smiled at that too.

He'd gone with a six-inch full-tang blade made of high carbon steel and a Scandinavian grind. It took him the better part of three months to settle on it—to find one that could send off a shower of sparks when struck against the right material. That meant finding one with a sharp ninety-degree edge that wasn't factory coated. He'd coated the blade with olive oil himself. They said it was preferable to the petroleum-based lubricants if you were going to use the knife to process food. He didn't have any such plans, but he couldn't rule it out. Anything could happen in the wilderness.

The full-tang design meant that the knife was one solid piece of steel, the handle screwed to either side of it so that there was no danger of the blade falling apart. If the handle broke, he could fashion another one easily enough.

But the toughest decision was on which grind to choose. He'd narrowed it down to either convex or Scandinavian, ultimately deciding on the latter. A convex blade was more resilient but harder to maintain in the wild and more difficult to use for finer tasks. So they said. What did he know? Scandinavian seemed to him a good compromise between the resilience of the convex and the brittleness of the sharper but thin hollow grind.

The knife felt good in his hand. Seemed a natural fit, like it was made for his grip alone. Maybe he and Joseph would come up with a name for it this week. He slid it into the sheath and snapped it shut. Put it aside.

Next he picked up the axe. He had been as meticulous in choosing the eighteen-inch hunter's axe as he had been the knife. It had a Scandinavian head and a hickory handle with a straight grain all the way through. It was considered one of the best compromises for all-around use; and since he had no idea what he was getting into, he figured "all around" was his best option. Joseph had helped him burn lines into the handle every half inch so that it could also double as a measuring stick. Not that he planned on doing a lot of measuring, but who knew. Maybe he'd try to build one of those shelters that were in the book.

He folded the leather axe mask over the head and set the tool beside the knife.

He shook his head. The last time he'd been to the woods (not counting the nearby lake that he and Joseph occasionally fished) was eight years ago when Agent Johnson had stuck him in that cabin in the mountains. That had been enough wilderness to last him the rest of his life. But he reminded himself that this was for Joseph. And a week of camping wasn't such a big price to pay for some quality father and son bonding. Not when taking into consideration what the boy had been through. What they'd both been through.

It took him five minutes to arrange all the equipment into categories—pockets, belt pouch, haversack, and pack. The stuff that he would carry in his pockets and the things that would go on his belt he put into a backpack. He'd put them on his person when they reached the campsite.

He went to the living room and folded the eight-by-eight-foot oilcloth tarp that was spread across the floor into thirds. Then he folded a queen-sized wool blanket in half and placed it on top of the tarp. Folded a twin-sized wool blanket in half and laid it over the queen. Then he began to place items on the blanket that wouldn't be immediately needed and could be rolled up inside the pack. Stuff like rope and stakes and spare socks.

He rolled it up and set it aside.

Next he packed the belt pouch with things like a waterproof flashlight and matches. Then the haversack. He set them beside the blanket roll and stole another glance at the time.

Fifteen minutes before Stacey was asleep.

The rucksack was made of canvas and had a small number of pockets. The books had warned against getting a backpack with too many zippers and compartments, because it could take too long to remember what you put in each pouch. Keep it simple, stupid.

He'd gotten the pack (most of the stuff, actually) at a military surplus store. With cash, of course. He didn't know if they were still on anyone's watchlist, but he didn't need any red flags going off by putting knives and axes on his credit card.

The waterproof bag went in first to keep the equipment from getting wet. Then it was one item at a time, each one getting crossed off his list as it went in. Folding saw, bush pot, skillet, notebook and pencils, hemp rope, repair kit, whetstone, parachute cord, first aid kit...

When he was all done, he tied the blanket roll to the top of the pack. Then he stood and looked over his work. *Jerry packed all this crap*, he thought.

Jerry.

No one had called him that in a long time. But it was that part of him that was always imagining some post-apocalyptic scenario where he'd have to live off the land (or some other, more realistic reason that would cause him to go off the grid) that wanted to see if he could do it. So he decided to pack for more than just setting up a tent and roasting marshmallows. Maybe an EMP would go off next week, and he and Joseph would have to survive on their own for the next ten years. Not a pleasant thought.

And neither was how fast Stacey's window was closing.

He started taking the equipment out to the car, beginning with two exercise mats and Joseph's little backpack the two of them had packed before dinner.

It took four trips, and on his last one, he saw Stacey's face appear in the bedroom window above the driveway. And then the upstairs lights went out.

He quickly finished arranging everything, making sure that Joseph would have plenty of room in the back seat, and shut the door. He ran inside.

In his haste, he hadn't noticed what he knocked off the passenger seat and out of the car while shifting the gear around.

JACK WENT UP THE stairs, hitting light switches off as he went. When he reached the top, he found a melodic whisper traveling down the hall and followed it to Joseph's room.

Joseph had started listening to movie scores at night a few years ago. Said it helped him sleep. Right now it was the late James Horner who was composing the soundtrack to his dreams. The Jackie Chan *Karate Kid* remake.

Jack bent over to turn off the bedside lamp and paused. The light was washing over Joseph's face in such a way that he seemed to be glowing. Jack straightened. Studied his boy. The way his hair was coming down over his eye (against Stacey's wishes, they were having a hair-growing competition). The slow, methodical way his chest rose with each breath. He wondered what he was dreaming about, if it was as climactic as the music.

"I love you, Joe," he whispered. He pulled the blankets up a little higher so that they reached his small shoulders and then kissed his head. "We're gonna have a great week."

Then his eyes drifted, as they often did, to the scar.

And every time it took him back to that moment, to Vadim holding Joseph in front of him and dragging the knife across his neck. He wondered if Joseph remembered anything about that day. He hoped not, which was why he never asked. Best not to stir the pools of memory if the memory wasn't already floating there on the surface.

He turned the bedside lamp off, and Luke Skywalker's blue lightsaber glowed from the wall clock across the room. According to Luke's saber, he only had two minutes left.

He was about to turn the soundtrack off, but then thought better of it. As he walked out of the room, he instead turned it up a couple of notches.

A smile spread across his face as he walked down the hallway. The music following after him was from a training scene, and in the present context it made him feel like he was in a parody. He felt like loosening up, taking a couple of jabs, doing some neck rolls.

When he entered the bedroom, he thought he could see Stacey under the covers, lying on her side, asleep. His heart sank. But then a voice sounded from behind him.

"About time," she said.

He turned and could just make her out in the light coming from the hallway. She was in a new black lace teddy, complete with garter and stockings.

For some reason the lace made him think of the lingerie he'd found while looking for something to wear in Donny's drawer.

The engagement ring...

It had taken years, and maybe a few cigarettes, to get over Donny's death, but every once in a while, the sting of it still surfaced, as it was starting to now.

Until Stacey stepped forward and started to unbutton his shirt.

YOU THINK YOU'LL MAKE it the whole week?" Stacey asked.

They were lying on their backs and staring up at the ceiling in the dark.

"I'm planning on it. But the shelter is just a little over a half mile from the campsite. If things get uncomfortable, we'll just pack up and hike there." He turned his head toward her. "Are you gonna be okay?"

"Yeah, I think I can manage here on my own."

"You know what I mean."

She turned onto her side. "No, I don't know what you mean."

He returned his gaze to the ceiling.

"What?" she pressed.

"Nothing."

She propped herself up onto an elbow as the elephants came parading into the bedroom. "Are you talking about—"

"Forget it. I'm sure you'll be fine." He reached his hand over and placed it on her thigh. She still had the lace on.

But she wouldn't let it go. Not now that the subject was broached. "What are you thinking?"

He sighed. "I'm thinking this is the first time that I'm leaving you. That you'll be alone."

"Is this Jerry I'm hearing?" she asked, amused and a little surprised.

"Maybe."

She put her hand on his chest. "It's been a long time since I've heard anything from him."

"I've been keeping him in the basement."

He looked over and saw the white of her teeth and knew she was smiling. It made him smile too. And he thought that maybe that was why the urge for a cigarette had come back—a subconscious reflex meant to keep his conspiracy theorist alter ego at bay. Because he knew what getting back into that mindset would mean, what it would do to his peace of mind. If people had named him after Mel Gibson's character in the *Conspiracy Theory* movie before, what would he be like after everything that had gone down eight years ago—when he'd found himself at the center of a CIA false-flag operation? No, ignorance now wasn't just bliss, it was essential. His wife was the daughter of KGB agents, ex-wife to a rogue SVR operative, and herself part of a CIA black op. Convincing Big Brother that they were happy to live normal, ignorant American lives was crucial to their being left alone. Hitting up the independent websites at 1a.m., checking out books on other American-made false-flag events, signing petitions to limit the scope of the NSA's surveillance system, and sharing WikiLeaks posts might just nudge them into the liability column. So he'd put Jerry in the basement and out of sight.

"If you're thinking what I think you're thinking," she said, lightly raking her fingernails over his skin, "I don't think you need to worry about it. I haven't spotted any activity in years."

"Would you tell me if you had?"

Silence drifted over them; her hand paused. "Depends," she finally said.

He nodded, able to appreciate her honesty.

She moved closer, putting one leg over top of his and an arm across his chest. "I can't believe you're going camping for a week." She nibbled his earlobe. "In the mountains."

"I know."

"What if there are bears?"

"As long as they aren't carrying AK-47s, we should be okay."

"What?"

"Kidding." But then he wondered if he was.

"Snakes, mountain lions, poison berries..." She giggled. "I'm sorry. I so can't see you out there. I give you three days max before you're going to the shelter or coming home."

"Think Joseph would be disappointed."

"No doubt."

"Okay, it's a bet."

"What is?"

"That I make it the whole time."

"And the stakes?"

He thought about it. Then lifted up the covers and pretended to look beneath them. "I can think of a few things."

"Okay. And if you don't make it, you need to start on the deck."

"What deck?"

"Exactly."

He groaned. "Fine."

Her teeth appeared again. "We'll have to change your name from Jerry to Jeremiah."

"As in Jeremiah Johnson?"

She ran her hand over his coming beard. "You're practically halfway there."

He laughed. "Yeah, right." Then he asked, "How do you know about that movie?"

"My mom had a thing for Robert Redford."

"Really?" He wondered if the Kremlin would been okay with one of their spies having the hots for an American actor, but didn't want to dampen the mood by bringing up the Motherland. He'd been very delicate when speaking about Viktoriya, mostly for Stacey's sake but also out of respect for the Russian countess. The last twenty minutes of her life had completely reshaped his view of her, and he thought the two of them could have gotten along just fine after clearing the air and taming all their elephants. Though he wasn't sure how things would have played out between her and Stacey...

He fell asleep and, for the first time in years, dreamed of bears.

The Story Continues In...

MAN IN THE WOODS

Eight years after the events of Man In The Water, Jack takes Joseph on a camping trip for some much needed father-son time. But when he wakes up to find Joseph missing from their tent, everything he thinks he knows about the past is suddenly thrown back into question. As Stacey finds herself in the midst of a sinister plot back home, Jack faces the wilderness and a father's worst fear in book two of the Jack and Stacey Green thrillers.

CALL TO ACTION

If you enjoyed this story, I would really appreciate you taking a quick moment to leave a review! That would be so helpful! And if you did leave a review, I'd love to hear from you so that I can thank you personally!

Also, if you'd like to be part of my street team, connect with me via my website jonhillwrites.com! And don't forget to get on the mailing list for your free ultimate beach read! Thanks so much! See you around!

-Jon

Free Book!

Visit www.jonhillwrites.com and join the mailing list for your free novella! This is the only way you can read this story. It is not for sale!

Also Available

The Jack & Stacey Green Thrillers
Man In The Water
Man In The Woods
Man In The Fire (forthcoming)
Standalone novels
My Wife Beth (forthcoming)
Seagull: A Novella of Avian Terror

Much more is on deck, including a new character series (that will merge The Jack and Stacey Green thrillers and My Wife Beth into the same world), episodes of a post-apocalyptic story along the lines of Seagull. A futuristic conspiracy set in Antarctica, and much more.

Be sure to visit jonhillwrites.com to get on the mailing list and get a free copy of

Seagull, to contact me, and for the inside scoop on current and upcoming projects!

About the Author

Jon Hill lives in Pennsylvania with his wife, children, and dog (princess) Leia. He's been on three cruises which helped inspire *Man In The Water*. He loves to read and write, preferably on stormy days, and spends too much time watching movies when he should be writing. He is an avid football fan and misses the days of pick-up tackle football and two-on-two sand volleyball. He still gets to play basketball on occasion, but he's not that good at it. He works out and hates running, but since his wife is a runner, he finds himself trying to impress her by delivering race times slower than their elementary school daughters. He can still beat them all in a sprint though, so at least there's that.

He is busy working on the next novel.

Milton Keynes UK
Ingram Content Group UK Ltd.
UKHW012258100524
442532UK00004B/101

9 780578 958699